One of Those Days . . .

He stopped walking about three feet from me as I stood next to my car.

He said raspingly, "You son-of-a-bitch!"

"Slow down," I warned him. "It's been a bad day. What's your beef, Ritter?"

"You," he said. "Put up your hands, you bastard."

"Come inside and talk quietly," I said, "or I'll send for the police."

"You'll send for the police? You haven't got any friends in this town, Callahan. Now put up your hands or crawl into your hole."

I turned and started for the manager's office and he moved quickly to put a hand on my shoulder and turn me around.

He had me turned with his left hand and his right arm was cocked for delivery. I suppose I could have moved inside of it and wrestled him to some kind of sanity, but the day had held too many frustrations.

I moved inside of his wild right, pushed him back, and threw a right of my own, a punch that carried the added weight of the day's humiliations.

SSSSSSSSSSSSSSSSSSSSSSSSSSSSSSSSSSSSSSSSSSSS

"Gault is coming on like the hottest kid in town."
—*Los Angeles Times*

"William Campbell Gault writes with passion, beauty, and with the ineffable madness which has previously been found only in Raymond Chandler."
—*Los Angeles Daily News*

COUNTY KILL

KILL

William Campbell Gault

CHARTER BOOKS, NEW YORK

This Charter Book contains the complete
text of the original hardcover edition.
It has been completely reset in a typeface
designed for easy reading, and was printed
from new film.

COUNTY KILL

A Charter Book / published by arrangement with
the author

PRINTING HISTORY
Simon and Schuster edition published 1962
Charter edition / April 1988

ISBN: 1-55773-017-2

Charter Books are published by The Berkley Publishing Group,
200 Madison Avenue, New York, New York 10016.
The name ''Charter'' and the ''C'' logo are trademarks
belonging to Charter Communications, Inc.

PRINTED IN THE UNITED STATES OF AMERICA

10 9 8 7 6 5 4 3 2 1

For John V. Pollitt
Ardent and incurable
READER

ONE

It was a hot October afternoon when the kid walked into my office. I had finished a case that morning and had seventeen hundred dollars in the bank. That isn't a lot of money, but it's a lot of money for me.

So I was solvent and not employed, and I guess that could be a reason for my misguided charity. Because there were two things wrong with this Lund business right from the start. Nobody was paying me and the kid lived in San Valdesto.

I was not a popular man in San Valdesto; very few outsiders were.

Of course, when he first walked in, I didn't know he was from San Valdesto. He was a stocky kid with bright brown eyes and a very dirty face.

"Brock Callahan, right?" he said. "You look just like your pictures."

I nodded. "And you—"

"Warren Temple Lund the Third," he answered. "Most people call me Bud."

In my mind a small bell tolled. Where had I heard or

read that name? And only recently, too. . . .

I asked, "What did you want, Bud—an autograph?"

He nodded, staring at me anxiously. "That—and—" he took a breath—"I thought you could phone my mom for me."

I sat up straighter. "Oh? And who is your mom?" I raised a hand quickly. "Don't answer. Any detective would know she is Mrs. Warren Temple Lund the Second."

He nodded.

The bell was ringing louder. *Lund, Lund, Lund.* . . . A subheadline came to mind—one I had glanced at on my way to breakfast this morning. I closed my eyes, trying to remember.

With my eyes still closed, I said, "You're not from around here, are you, Bud? You don't live in Beverly Hills."

"Not any more," he admitted. "We used to. I thought maybe my dad had come down to the old house. But there's nobody there. The furniture is there but—"

"And the police are looking for you," I interrupted, and opened my eyes.

We stared at each other. He took another deep and shuddering breath. *And for your father,* I thought, but didn't say.

He said again, "I thought you could call my mom." There was a quick glint of tears in his eyes.

"Steady, soldier," I said gently. "It's no time for tears. Just have a chair and we'll talk this out. Are you hungry?"

He sat down and nodded. "I had a hamburger yesterday noon. I only had enough money for bus fare. I thought my dad would be here and—" He stared at the floor.

"I'll get us some food," I said, and picked up the phone.

The drugstore where I usually ate lunch had a food-delivery service, and I called it. I ordered three hamburgers and two double malts and told the man to hurry. My own light lunch was two hours behind me and I didn't want the boy to eat alone.

As I put down the phone, I asked, "How old are you, Bud?"

"I'll be twelve in a couple months," he said.

"And yesterday noon," I said, "you left school at the lunch hour and your mom hasn't seen you since, has she?"

He stared at the floor in embarrassment.

"You came here all the way from San Valdesto," I said. "That's ninety miles, Warren Temple Lund the Third."

"Eighty-seven," he corrected me, "and all freeway. It's not much of a trip."

"In this morning's paper," I went on gravely, "you're a headline."

He continued to look at the floor. "I didn't see it."

Silence.

He looked up and his bright brown eyes were still wet. "I wanted to find my dad. Is there something wrong with that?"

"Nothing," I agreed. "Why didn't you tell your mother you wanted to see your dad?"

"I did. A million times. He doesn't live with us, you know. He hasn't lived with us for three months. But he'd come to see me and take me out on the boat. But not lately. Mom said he was on a trip. He could write, couldn't he?"

I kept my voice quiet. "So you skipped school yesterday and took a bus down here without telling anybody. And now all the police in this end of the state are looking for you. By now, perhaps even the FBI has been called in."

"The FBI?" He stared fearfully. "Why?"

"How does your mother know you weren't kidnaped? The FBI moves in on kidnapings, Warren."

"Kidnaping," he said bleakly. "Who'd want me?"

My throat was tight and my voice too shrill. "Don't talk like that. Anybody with any sense would want you. What kind of silly remark was that?"

"You don't have to holler," he said glumly. He stared at the top of my desk. "Do we have to call the police now?"

"No," I told him. "If we call the police, the newspapers will hear about it. And once you get the reporters into something like this it gets all messed up. We'll just call your mother on the quiet. *After* we eat."

The food came soon after that, and while we ate he told me he had slept in the garage of his former home last night and tried to break into the house without success.

"Why didn't you look me up last night?"

"I thought maybe my dad would come to the house. I wanted to be there if he did."

"Didn't you believe your mother when she said he was on a trip?"

He didn't answer, giving a lot of attention to his food.

"Has she lied to you before?"

He shrugged.

We ate in silence for a few seconds. Then, in a tight voice, he said, "Wouldn't he write to me if he was on a trip?"

I said nothing, there being nothing to say.

"Wouldn't he? *Damn it,* wouldn't he?"

"Don't swear," I said softly. "Simmer down, Warren. I never met your father. I don't know what he'd do."

His hand holding the malted trembled. "Would *you* write to me if you were my father and you were on a trip?"

"Eat that second hamburger," I said sternly. "It's too much for me. C'mon, eat it!"

He sighed and began to eat again.

I asked, "What brought you to my office?"

"I knew you were a detective now. I knew I could trust you. My dad used to take me to the Coliseum when we lived here. I saw you play seven times your last year with the Rams. My dad said you're the greatest guard that ever lived. *Anywhere,* he said."

Oh, boy. . . . All that blarney and me with seventeen hundred in the bank. I was hooked.

A silence, while he studied me. Then, shyly, "How much do you charge?"

I told him sternly, "A hundred dollars a day and expenses. But I'm not going to charge you that just for phoning your mother."

He looked at his half-eaten hamburger and his voice was even quieter. "I didn't mean that. I meant, if you went looking for my dad, how much would you charge a kid under twelve?"

Didn't he know the police were looking for his father right now? Evidently not. I said, "Don't con me, Warren Lund." I wiped my hands on a paper napkin and reached for the phone. "What's your number in San Valdesto?"

He gave it to me and I called person to person for Mrs. Warren Lund in San Valdesto.

I could hear a man's gruff voice answer the phone. The operator asked for Mrs. Lund and the man said, "She's not available right now. I'll take the call."

I told the operator that would be O.K.

"Hello, hello," he said irritably. "James Ritter here."

I ignored the phone for a second and asked Bud quietly, "Who's James Ritter?"

"A friend of my mother's," he said. "A *creep.*"

To the man on the phone, I said, "Is there no way I could speak with Mrs. Lund? It's very important. I have some news about her son."

"News? You mean he's there?"

"That's right, Mr. Ritter. He's here, safe and sound. Will you put Mrs. Lund on, please?"

"She's under sedation," he said hoarsely. "Now Mr. Who-ever-you-are, I've had about enough nonsense. You put Warren on the phone and I'll talk with him."

"Slow down, Ritter," I said. "I'm a friend of Bud's and he's O.K. He wasn't kidnaped; he ran away and wound up here. I'll see if he wants to speak with you."

I turned to look at Bud and he was shaking his head no, no, no. He left his chair and went to a far corner of the room, his face set, his hands shaking.

I said soothingly, "Mr. Ritter, you'll have to trust me. I don't think any of us want any publicity about this. So I'll just pile Bud into my car and drive up there. If we let the police in on it, the papers will be alerted. None of us want that, do we?"

"Mister," he said harshly, "I don't know who the hell you are, but unless you want more trouble than you can handle, you put Bud on the phone right now."

"We'll play it my way," I said calmly. "We'll be leaving in a few minutes. We should be there in an hour and a half to two hours. *Please* don't call in the police. This boy has had too damned much publicity already." I hung up.

Warren Temple Lund the Third sighed and said gratefully, "I knew I could trust you. My dad said they call you The Rock because you are. He said you're—"

"A sucker," I finished for him. "I was going to take my girl along on the trip, but I guess I'd better not."

He looked at me quizzically.

"The police," I explained. "I told that Ritter not to call them, but he doesn't sound like a man who'd take outside advice. It could be sticky going up there for an hour or two."

He opened his mouth and closed it. Then, "Why didn't Mom come to the phone?"

"She had to take something so she could rest. You worried her, Bud. She's under sedation."

"Huh!" he said. "She's probably drunk. That's all she does since Dad left—drink, drink, drink."

Another of our silences. We stared at each other, and

finally I asked, "Do you live right in San Valdesto or outside of town?"

"In Montevista," he said. "That's on this side."

And Slope Ranch on the other, I thought. Between them lived the plain people, the light drinkers.

I phoned Jan at her shop and she was in. I told her, "I'll have to break that date for dinner. I'm going out of town."

"Alone?" she asked suspiciously.

"Not alone. With a young friend of mine. We're going up to San Valdesto."

A silence, a long silence, and then, very softly, "Brock, you don't mean Glenys Christopher's nephew? June's boy?"

"If he is, I didn't know it," I said. "Jan, silence is very important now. Please don't say a word to *anybody.*"

Another pause. "All right. Has his mother been notified?"

"Yup. Maybe I'll be back tonight. If you have a light on, I'll stop in."

"It'll be on all night," she said. "And Brock—watch your temper, won't you? Those police in San Valdesto—"

"I'll be careful." I hung up.

Glenys Christopher was a client of Jan's and she had been a client of mine, some years back, on my first case.

I asked Bud, "Don't you have an aunt in this town?"

He nodded. "Aunt Glenys. I don't like her. You're not going to call *her*, are you?"

"Not if you don't want me to. Isn't she married?"

"She was married," he said dully. "But not for long, and she got her own name back. It was like a divorce, only it wasn't."

"An annulment?"

"That's what they called it." His face tightened. "Mom says she can't get one of those; she'd have to get a divorce. Brock, why don't people stay married?"

"A lot of people do. San Valdesto and Beverly Hills just

seem to have more people who don't. Is your mother thinking of getting a . . ."

I couldn't finish. He nodded, his eyes on the floor.

I said, "Let's go. Your mother will be worried."

We went down to my ancient flivver and drove over to the filling station. I filled the tank to the brim; gasoline was much more expensive in San Valdesto.

We took the Valley route through the dry, gray hills and didn't see the ocean until we were past Ventura. Bud sat glumly in the seat next to me, offering no conversational openings, and no remarks came to me that seemed likely to brighten his mood.

A drinking mother and a missing father. . . . *Who'd* want me? Sociologists are so concerned with the rise of juvenile delinquency. It was the adult delinquency that gave me the shakes.

The ocean came into view and it had some blue in it for a change. The gray clay cliffs to the right, the flat ocean to the left, and a bleak moodiness in the car.

I said, "Bud, adults aren't easy to understand. They get all messed up and mess up other lives, too. You have to live *your* life. Your life is the important one; most of it's ahead of you."

"Sure," he said tonelessly.

"You're your own best friend," I went on dumbly. "You'll find other friends you can trust, but it takes time. Don't try to hurry it; it takes patience."

"Sure," he said once more.

I gave him a few more miles of silence and then asked, "How long since you've heard from your dad?"

"A couple weeks. I'd always see him at least three times a week."

A couple weeks. . . . The police hadn't started looking for him until last night, when a man named Johnny Chavez had been found dead in a cabin in the hills high above San Valdesto. Johnny and Lund had supposedly gone on the trip together. Evidently Bud hadn't seen this morning's headlines.

He said, "Couldn't you look for him? I've only got thirty-two dollars saved, but Mom would pay you, I'll bet. She'd do *that* for me, wouldn't she?"

"Your dad must pay her money for your support," I pointed out. "She ought to know where he is."

Bud shook his head. He seemed embarrassed. "I don't think Pop has any money of his own."

I had made the natural mistaken assumption that a man with three names and a number was wealthy. I had forgotten that many poor but pretentious people had adopted the pattern.

But Bud's mother was a Christopher and I *knew* they were wealthy. I said, "When I met your Aunt Glenys I thought she only had that younger brother. Who else is there?"

"Just Aunt Glenys and Uncle Bob and Mom," he answered. "Mom was married when she was seventeen."

"I see. And what does your dad do?"

"When we lived in Beverly Hills, he had a filling station. That's where he met Mom. Dad had this hot rod and Mom had her Mercedes, see, and they used to tease each other, and one day they had this race and Mom tipped over and broke her leg and Pop found out then, see, how much he loved her and—" He broke off. "It's just like a story, isn't it?"

With a detergent commercial, I thought. I thought of the austere, black-haired, composed, and beautiful Glenys Christopher. With a hot-rodder in the family. . . .

I asked, "What did your Aunt Glenys think about the marriage?"

"I guess she wasn't for it. But Uncle Bob was. Uncle Bob and Pop get along great."

When I'd known Uncle Bob, he had just been graduated from Beverly Hills High School, a hotshot halfback weighing the football scholarship offers which he didn't need.

Bud said, "Uncle Bob thinks you're great, too."

"I know. He told me. What's he doing now?"

"He's a lawyer. In San Francisco."

From a cynical high-school halfback to a San Francisco lawyer. That was quite a climb. Unlike Callahan, Bobby hadn't wasted his football reputation.

Silence as we approached Carpinteria. We were past it when Bud said, "I don't want to go home. Boy, I'll *get* it when I come home!"

"You can't run forever, Bud," I told him.

Another silence and then, "Couldn't you stay with us for a while? We've got lots of rooms."

Brother! The father image, Brock (The Rock) Callahan. The hero, the knight with piano legs. What could I say?

I said what I shouldn't have said. Because I had seventeen hundred in the bank and his aunt had been my first client. Because I'm a sucker for kids, I said, "Maybe it would be better if I got right to work on finding your father."

Committed, now. Bigmouth Callahan. No fee, no retainer, no sense, no anything but my big mouth and the faith of a dirty-faced kid with family trouble.

Bud sighed happily and the flivver murmured contemptuously and I thought about Mrs. Warren Temple Lund the Second, who had married at seventeen—married a hot-rodder who ran a filling station in Beverly Hills. He had probably used only two names and no number until he had met a Christopher.

I asked Bud, "Did your father call his filling station the Warren Temple Lund the Second's Filling Station?"

"Nah. He just called it Skip's. That's what everybody calls him—Skip. My Aunt Glenys gave that dopey name to the newspapers when Dad and Mom eloped. Aunt Glenys is kind of—well—" He broke off, abashed.

"I know exactly what you mean," I comforted him, "but you have to admit she is a beautiful woman."

"Maybe," he said. "Isn't Miss Bonnet your girl? Isn't she the lady that fixed up Aunt Glenys' house—you know, a—a—"

"An interior decorator," I supplied. "Yes, she's my girl. Do you think she's pretty?"

"She's a lot prettier than Aunt Glenys," he said stoutly. "And peppier, too. How come you're not married yet?"

"I—uh—don't make the kind of money Miss Bonnet needs to maintain the kind of living she likes. The way things are in my business, Bud, I may *never* make that kind of money."

"Money, money, money." He sighed. "Is that all grown-ups ever think about? It's all they ever talk about."

"It's all most of them know, Bud," I explained. "That's why I want you to enjoy what you're going through now. Once you're out of high school, life just isn't the same any more. It gets real dull."

"Couldn't you be a coach?" he persisted. "Couldn't you play with the Rams again and have enough money to marry Miss Bonnet?"

"No," I said. "Son, I am what I am and not a bit ashamed of it."

The Montevista turnoff now, and I swung the flivver that way and we climbed the ramp in a stiff silence.

At the top, Bud said, "I wasn't criticizing; I was only asking. Turn right on that road next to the filling station."

He directed me from there along a winding, black-top road bordered in eucalypti and palms, past estates and cottages, past a country club, to a driveway flanked by stucco pillars.

We turned in here. The pillars were chipped and rain-streaked, the driveway pitted and long and poorly maintained. The lawn was a dried-out gray, dotted with succulents. If Mrs. Lund had a gardener, he wasn't doing his job.

Ahead of us now we could see the house, two-story, old and massive, faintly Norman, and newly painted. There was a green Pontiac station wagon on the drive before the front door. A red Porsche two-seater was parked behind it. There were no police cars in sight.

But as we stepped from the car the law erupted from the shrubbery—two uniformed men and a man in plain clothes— and the uniformed men had their guns out and pointing straight at my belly.

And the man out of uniform barked sharply, "Damn you, stand right where you are!"

I stood like a statue, lacking a wreath.

And Bud said, "For criyi, are you guys off your rocker? This is Brock (The Rock) Callahan, for criyi!"

≋≋≋≋≋≋≋≋≋≋≋≋ *TWO* ≋≋≋≋≋≋≋≋≋≋≋≋

THE UNIFORMED MEN were troopers, borrowed from the State Patrol station on the other side of town. The man in plain clothes was a detective-sergeant out of San Valdesto Headquarters and not actually in his jurisdiction, as this was county.

But he was a friend of James Edward Ritter's, and Mr. Ritter appeared to be more than a friend of Mrs. Lund's. Ritter had called him in after clearing it with the Sheriff's Department.

His name was Sergeant Bernard Vogel and he explained all this to me carefully and politely in the living room of the Lund home. He was a man of medium height and impressive width and his politeness didn't fool me for a second. He was a sharp, tough pro, and I would guess he could get real mean if he had to.

Bud and his mother had gone through a damp reunion. James Edward Ritter had watched it quietly, making his own judgments, I was sure. He was a man almost my size, but stuffier and a shade older. He kept glancing our way as Vogel talked with me in one corner of the immense room.

When Vogel finished, I said, "I'm glad to see there aren't any reporters around."

"The Los Angeles papers weren't notified about your call," he explained. "There'll be a local man who may want some answers when we get down to Headquarters."

"We?" I said. "My job's finished, Sergeant."

"Yes. But you certainly won't object to a few questions, will you?"

"About what and from whom?"

"About young Warren and from us. The Los Angeles papers and the wire services can pick up their copy from the local paper. There'll be one reporter with a photographer from the local paper down at the station. We're doing the best we can about publicity, but there's only so much we can expect after this morning's headline, of course."

I said nothing, thinking.

"Well . . . ?" he asked.

"How about the sheriff?" I stalled. "Isn't he going to be miffed about you city slickers getting all the ink?" I lowered my voice so Bud wouldn't overhear. "The way I understand it, Johnny Chavez wasn't a city kill either."

He frowned and inhaled heavily.

"I don't want to make any enemies," I explained hastily. "I may be around town for a few days and I can't afford enemies."

His frown deepened and his voice was gruffer. "Around town? Why?"

I shrugged.

"Callahan," he warned me, "we'll get along a lot better if you're completely frank with me."

"All right, Sergeant. It's because of Bud—of young Warren. I promised him I'd help find his father. I guess he doesn't know about this suspicion of murder bit yet. He doesn't know *you're* looking for his father."

"We can't keep it from him forever," he said. "He can read. You do a lot of charity work, do you, Callahan?"

"Never. But . . . well, Bud's a fan of mine, and I knew his aunt at one time—she was my first client—and . . ." I sighed. "So I'm a sucker for kids and I happen to have a couple bucks in the bank at the moment. Is there some reason why you don't want me around town?"

His face stiffened. "Now what in hell did that mean?"

"You tell me. You've been acting like a cop in a TV show. My reputation is pretty sound in and around Los Angeles, Sergeant."

"We don't need any smog-town help up here," he said flatly. "We wouldn't have half the troubles we do have if it wasn't for the smog-towners who are moving in here."

Hick-town resentment, provincial petulance—who could argue against an attitude that knot-headed? I said nothing.

And then Mrs. Lund was coming over with Bud, her arm around his shoulders. "I'm sorry, Mr. Callahan, that I haven't been able to thank you until now. It's been—hectic."

"You're welcome," I said. "I guess I'll be leaving now, Mrs. Lund. The sergeant wants me down at Headquarters."

She smiled and looked at the sergeant as I looked at her. She had chestnut hair and deep-blue eyes and a candid, direct gaze. She looked like the All-American girl, too many cocktails later. There was a slackness in her face too old for her twenty-nine years.

She asked Vogel, "No trouble, Bernie, is there? Mr. Callahan isn't in any kind of trouble, I'm sure."

He put on his customer's smile. "Routine, June. Are you a member of the Callahan fan club, too?"

Her chin lifted and the slackness was gone from her face. "Skip is. I've only heard of him through Skip. And Bud here." She turned to me. "Could you come back for dinner? Bud wants it, so much!"

"I can make it, thank you," I said, and looked at Vogel. "If I'm free by that time."

He took a deep breath, looked at me and at Mrs. Lund, and nodded heavily in assent.

I went down in my car; Sergeant Vogel followed in a Department car. At Headquarters he took me right into the chief's office.

Chief of Police Chandler Harris had snow-white hair and a pudgy face and a voice like crushed rock in a rusty bucket. He pointed at a chair, told me to sit down, and nodded at Vogel.

Vogel left the room and Harris leaned back in his chair to stare at me. It was possible that he was trying to intimidate me, but that had been tried by major-leaguers. I stared back blandly.

Finally he admitted grudgingly, "I checked you out while Vogel was talking to you. Both in Beverly Hills and Los Angeles. You check out pretty solid for a peeper."

"I'm glad you didn't call Santa Monica," I said. "I'm not a peeper, Chief. I'm a licensed and bonded private investigator. Let's not get our semantics muddled."

"A smog-town smart aleck," he said. "College man, huh?"

"Stanford," I admitted.

He continued to stare, appraising me.

I said quietly, "Sergeant Vogel told me the local paper would want to ask some questions. Will that be soon? Mrs. Lund is expecting me for dinner."

He opened his hands and looked at the palms. He studied the top of his desk. I waited.

Finally he said, in a quieter voice, "We'll have to compose our story first."

I frowned in artful innocence. "Story . . . ?"

His voice less quiet. "Of course. Do we want to tell those nosy people that the Lunds are getting a divorce, that Jim

Ritter was the one who called us in, that Mrs. Lund was drunk when you phoned? Do we have to spread all that out for the world to read?"

"Absolutely not," I agreed. "The kid's got it rough enough already."

"The kid?" he said doubtfully.

"Warren Temple Lund the Third," I explained. ''*My* client.''

"Oh." He nodded. "Sure. Fan of yours, isn't he? Never could see that football. Baseball's more to my taste."

I said nothing. It was a free country.

So we dreamed up a gasser and called in the local newshawk and his Brownie buddy. And one more—a man from the local TV station.

The way we explained it, Bud had gone to pay a surprise visit to his Aunt Glenys in Beverly Hills. (Vogel had already alerted her.) But, we went on, his Aunt Glenys hadn't been home, so Bud had wandered around town and finally looked up his old idol, a friend of his Aunt Glenys', former Stanford All-American and Ram immortal, Brock (The Rock) Callahan, presently an impeccably respectable private investigator.

The name of Bud's father was not mentioned in this account we presented, and Harris made it clear in answering the reporter's questions that Bud's trip and his father's disappearance had no connection.

He lied about that, and I substantiated it. We were lying allies for the moment, and I could hope that that would give me a few unharassed days in San Valdesto.

I didn't bring up the subject, though. So long as he didn't, there would be no reason why I couldn't hang around town, having not been told not to, if you follow me. Our mutual lie made us uneasy allies—more than I had hoped for on entering his office. When the situation worsened, I would have to come up with something stronger, if possible.

Vogel wasn't in sight when I came out of the chief's office, and I didn't wait to look him up. I bought a local paper and drove over to the north side of town, to a motel I had stayed at before called the Deauville Dobe.

The summer rates were no longer in effect and I got a nice unit near the pool. I could write this off as a vacation; how else could I justify it without being sentimental?

It was now six o'clock, but I phoned Jan at her shop and she was still working.

I told her, "I'll be here for a couple of days. I thought you could pick up some of my clothes for me and come up to share my vacation."

"I can't make it," she said ruefully. "I'm just starting the Kesselring place and it takes all day every day. Maybe I could come up Saturday night and stay over Sunday."

This was Thursday. I said, "Do that. And could you ship some clothes up to me?"

"Wait," she said. "I think Glenys is coming up to be with her sister and she could—oh, no!"

"No, what?"

"If she brought up your clothes, she'd know I have a key to your apartment."

"So? Would it make her jealous? She wouldn't care."

"Oh, shut up! You're so vulgar."

I was vulgar. *She* had the key, but *I* was vulgar. I said nothing.

A silence on the line for a few seconds, and then she said, "I suppose I could tell her the superintendent let me in. O.K., that's what I'll do. What's your address up there?"

"I'm staying at the Deauville Dobe. But it would be better if she brought the clothes to her sister's house. I'll pick them up there."

I didn't want to put an image into Jan's mind, a mental

picture of Glenys Christopher coming into my cozy motel room, a grip full of my clothes in her hand. Jan has an extremely unreasonable imagination.

"All right," she agreed. "And, Brock . . . why are you staying there? Did June Lund hire you?"

"Well," I stalled, "not exactly. You see, the boy—well, he doesn't know his father is wanted by the police—not yet—and I thought maybe—"

"Brock Callahan," she said acidly, "those people are *rich*. If you want to do charity work, do it for the *poor*. You make me sick!"

"Honey," I said soothingly, "this is a little vacation for me. Now you come up Saturday night. I miss you."

"I'll try. Remember, now; don't be a damned fool."

A financial fool, she meant. I promised I wouldn't.

I showered and read the local paper. The story of Johnny Chavez was there; he had been found by a sheriff's deputy making a check of the isolated cabins that dotted the various peaks in the area. According to his sister, Mary Chavez, Johnny had gone up there with Skip Lund on a hunting trip. What they were hunting in October Miss Chavez was not prepared to state.

Chavez had been killed with a .30-.30. That's a deer-rifle caliber. Could they have been hunting deer? The story ended by stating that Warren Lund was being sought for questioning in connection with the "shooting." It hadn't been established as murder yet.

I climbed into the flivver and headed for Montevista.

As I came up the long, bumpy driveway my headlights picked up my client in front of the garage. He was putting his bike away.

"Hi," he said. "Do you know who won today? That dopey paper boy forgot to leave us one."

The Series was on in New York. I said, "The Yankees,

in the tenth. Glad to be home again?"

"I guess." He glanced toward the lighted living-room window. "Mom's already had a couple of drinks. Martinis." He made a face.

"It's the cocktail hour," I said cheerfully. I put a hand on his shoulder. "Someday you'll be old enough to drink. It's—like medicine to some people."

"Sure," he said.

What do you tell them? In the reflected light from the living-room window I looked at my client and he at me. *Adults,* I thought; *damn them all!*

I ruffled his hair. "Remember what I told you: you're your own best friend. Let's go in and join the party."

We went up and through the entry hall and into the bright living room. June Lund was sitting on an enormous, curving sofa of chartreuse silk, her slim legs curled up under her, both hands encasing her Martini. Next to the fireplace, whisky and ice in his glass, James Edward Ritter stood like the lord of the manor. For some reason this man annoyed me. He was such an unctuous square.

"Hello," June said, and "Good evening," Ritter said, and I nodded and smiled at them both.

"Drink?" she asked.

"I rarely touch the hard stuff," I told her. "I'd appreciate a glass of beer."

"Of course," she said. "Any special brand?"

There was only a slight slurring of her sibilants and very little glaze in her eyes, but I had a feeling that she was carefully avoiding any appearance of drunkenness.

The maid had come in and was waiting for my order.

"I favor Einlicher," I told June Lund, "but I don't often find it."

She looked at the maid and the woman shook her head.

"Miller, then?" I asked, and the maid nodded and went out.

For a moment all three of them were looking at me. It was then that Bud said proudly, "Mr. Callahan's going to find Pop."

Both Ritter and Mrs. Lund looked startled, but I thought there was another emotion on the face of Ritter—annoyance.

June Lund said blankly, "Find?" She stared worriedly at Bud.

"What's wrong with that?" Bud asked belligerently. "He can tell him to write, can't he, when he finds him? Then I'll know what Pop's doing."

His mother said steadily, "Didn't I tell you he was on a trip? Do you think I'm lying to you?"

Bud flushed and studied the carpeting on the floor.

His mother glanced at Ritter and then said gently to her son, "It's time to wash up, tiger. We'll be eating soon."

He went out quietly, taking my heart along. The maid brought my beer.

When the maid had left, Ritter said, "That boy needs discipline, June. He's insolent."

I looked at him over my beer. He met my glance and the contempt in his eyes probably matched mine.

June Lund said quietly to me, "We've kept the papers from him so far. But he'll have to go to school tomorrow and the other children will know." She sighed. "His father has found some strange friends up here, Mr. Callahan." She paused again, glanced at Ritter, and continued in a near whisper. "One of his *very special* friends is Mary Chavez, the sister of the man who was killed."

Ritter said sharply, "Damn it, June, you're talking to a private investigator! Show a little discretion."

I said to him, *"Private* is the definitive word there, Mr.

Ritter." I turned back to her. "Do you know where your husband is?"

She shook her head slowly, staring moodily at her drink. "I lied to Bud about the trip. I had to tell him something." Her chin came up defiantly. "Skip Lund hasn't been a husband for six months, and he's been a bad father this past month."

"Oh, God!" Ritter said. "June, please! Don't you realize the ammunition you're giving this man?"

I felt a tremor in my knee and a tightness at the base of my neck. I tried to keep my voice calm. "Mr. Ritter, I'd appreciate it if you'd stay out of this conversation. If Mrs. Lund wants a character reference, she can get one from any of half a dozen chiefs of police or her own sister, for whom I once worked."

He said coolly, "That's a good idea. We'll get the references first, and then if Mrs. Lund still wants to reveal family secrets to you, we'll arrange a time when she hasn't had three double Martinis. Is that reasonable?"

He was a cutie, this one. I almost admired him. I couldn't think of anything wrong with his suggestion.

But June Lund said, *"We,* Jim? Are you acting as my attorney? I didn't know you were qualified."

His face stiffened. "I'm acting in your interests, June. And I'm sober."

"That's your major fault," she said. "You're *always* sober." She sighed and smiled bleakly at me. "Mr. Callahan, I have no idea where Skip Lund is. I started divorce proceedings three weeks ago."

 *THREE*

IT WAS AN uncomfortable dinner. Bud and I found some communication, the World Series and the football fortunes of U.C.L.A. and Southern Cal. The Rams and Stanford were topics too painful for me to discuss this season.

Mrs. Lund and her friend(?) maintained an absolute minimum of dialogue; he was still miffed at her revelations to me and she had clearly resented his unsolicited advice. If this was the best she could do as a substitute for her missing husband, it indicated a very low quota of eligible males in this tight little town.

So what business was it of mine? Warren Temple Lund the Second and Third were my business, and the love life of June Christopher Lund (if any) would have to remain her problem.

When the meal was finished, Mrs. Lund suggested that we have our coffee in the living room. We were heading that way when Bud asked me if I knew anything about bikes. His handle bars were loose, he said.

I excused myself and went outside with him.

There was nothing wrong with his handle bars; he had

simply wanted to talk with me privately. He asked, "What did my mom tell you? Did she tell you anything?"

I said carefully, "Nothing that will help. I'll check around town tomorrow. Maybe Sergeant Vogel knows something."

"He's no friend of Pop's, that Sergeant Vogel," Bud told me. "He's Mr. Ritter's buddy."

"Buddy?"

"Sure. They went to high school together. Do you like Mr. Ritter?"

"I—uh—don't know much about him, Bud. We'd better go back in."

We had turned toward the house when the headlights flashed in from the direction of the road. I said, "Let's wait. That might be your Aunt Glenys, and she's bringing up my clothes."

"Aunt Glenys?" he said. He didn't sound happy.

It was a big black Continental. It came whispering in under the floodlight of the yard and parked behind my faded flivver.

The tall, slim figure that stepped out from behind the wheel was familiar. And then her jet hair glinted in the overhead light and I said, "Hello, again."

"Brock Callahan," she said. "It's been a long time, hasn't it? Your grip is on the rear seat."

She held the door open; I reached in and took my bag. She was standing close to me and her perfume was expensive and disturbing.

She looked down at Bud. "And how are you, traveler?"

"O.K.," he said. "Fine, thank you."

"All the way to Beverly Hills," she said gently, "and you didn't even look up your Aunt Glenys. Am I not a friend of yours, Warren Temple Lund the Third?"

He stared at the ground and said nothing. There was a shadow over him, a bird-of-paradise tree that blocked out the light from the house. He seemed lost in the blackness.

Glenys sighed and looked sadly at me.

"I hear Bobby's a lawyer now," I said. "He turned out well for a halfback, didn't he?"

She nodded, still looking at Bud. "Aren't we friends? Aren't you glad to see me, Bud?"

"Sure," he said. "Sure. Why not? Hi."

"Hi," she said.

I put my bag into the flivver and we walked up to the front door together. As we drew closer we could hear June and Ritter arguing about something, and their voices were harsh.

Glenys muttered under her breath as Bud preceded us into the room. Bud said, "Aunt Glenys is here, Mom."

June Lund was back on the silk sofa, her feet under her once more, a small liqueur glass in her hand. "Glen!" she said excitedly, and started to rise.

Her feet were tangled and the drink tilted, spilling over the front of her dress and dripping onto the sofa.

Glenys froze, Ritter mumbled something I didn't catch, and Bud stared at her in abject shame. Then his eyes misted and he ran from the room and out the front door.

I left the others and went after my client.

I caught up to him just before he got to the end of the driveway. He was sobbing and he tried to squirm free of my grip.

"Easy, Bud," I soothed him.

"Drunk," he said hoarsely. "She's drunk! Why does she have to drink?"

"Her feet were tangled," I said. "It wasn't the liquor, boy. She didn't expect to see her sister so soon and she got excited. You're jumping to conclusions, Bud."

"Sure," he said. "Oh, *sure!*" He sniffed and rubbed his nose with the back of one hand.

From the lighted front porch now, Ritter called, "Callahan? You got the boy there?"

"Everything's all right," I called. "We're having a talk, a *private* business talk. We'll be in in a minute."

"His mother wants him in right now," he said, and started down our way.

"We're coming," I said. "We don't need any help."

He continued toward us. I must admit now that I was ashamed of the anger that started to boil in me, the almost adolescent rage. This pompous coupon clipper triggered the worst in me.

The way he was heading, I had a feeling he meant to take Bud's hand and either lead him or drag him into the house. And I was determined that that would not happen.

"Come here, Bud," he said roughly, and started to that side of me, his hand out to take Bud's.

I stepped between them and he bumped into me and stumbled.

He backed off a half step, breathing hard, studying me angrily.

"We can make it without help," I said. "I don't want any trouble with you, Ritter, and if you're wise you'll see we don't have any."

"Why—you," he stuttered; "you—you—"

"Yes?" I said quietly. "Say the magic word and go into orbit. One more word will do it."

Silence, and Bud broke it. He said in a high voice, "Why don't you go home? Nobody wants you around here anyway."

He stared at Bud and at me and said, "Your mother will hear about your insolence, young man." He turned his back on us and headed for the house.

"What a creep!" Bud said quietly. "Jeepers, why is he always hanging around here?"

I didn't answer. Who could explain adult taste to an intelligent child? We walked without further dialogue back to the house.

Glenys met us at the door. She said, "Bud, it's time for bed. Go in and say good night to your mother."

He said stubbornly, "I don't want to talk to her at all."

Glenys looked hopelessly at me. I said, "Bud, go in and be polite to your mother or I'll head back to Los Angeles tonight."

He looked up at me fearfully, gritted his teeth, and went ahead of us into the living room.

Glenys stood where we were for a moment and whispered, "Has my sister been drinking much this evening?"

"I caught her on her last one. According to Ritter, she had three double Martinis before dinner. That wouldn't make her an alcoholic."

"She has the potential to become one," Glenys said quietly. "Did you have trouble with Jim outside?"

"Words," I said. "No trouble. He's kind of a—dominant type, isn't he?"

"I don't know much about him," she said. "He comes from a very good family up here."

"Good or *rich?*"

She sighed. "Oh, yes, I'd forgotten. Callahan, the professional peasant. Class-conscious Callahan."

"And Glenys Christopher," I answered, "the professional socialite. You changed Skip Lund's name for him, I understand."

She flushed. She glared at me.

I said, "We'd better go in or they'll think we're necking."

"God," she said wearily, and we went back to the living room.

Bud was leaving as we came in. I told him, "I'll phone you tomorrow, boss. I'll keep in touch."

"O.K.," he said, and waved a good night.

Why wasn't I married, so I could have a boy like that? Because Jan was so absurd about solvency—that was why.

In the living room I said, "Thank you for the fine dinner, Mrs. Lund. I guess it would be better all around if I took off now."

"Suit yourself," she said. "*I* get along with you."

Ritter said nothing, looking grim. Glenys said, "You don't know him as I do. Good night, Brock."

"Good night, Miss Christopher," I said coolly. "Good night, all."

I was to the archway that led to the entry hall when Glenys said, "If we need you, where can we reach you?"

"At the Deauville Dobe," I told her. "The winter rates are now in effect."

June was the only one who laughed.

The road that led back to the highway was narrow and winding, overhung with trees, and deep in moving shadows as the headlights' beams struck at different angles. Gate posts glimmered like tombstones in a restricted cemetery, half lost in the heavy foliage.

Montevista, the land of the drinking dead. As I came up the ramp to the highway again, the lights of traffic were reassuring, the blat of the big diesels comforting.

At the Deauville Dobe the tourists were already asleep, the adulterers drinking their way to the big moment. It was only ten o'clock and I wasn't sleepy. I turned on the TV to a Los Angeles news commentator.

His report on Bud's adventure came near the end of his fifteen minutes and basically followed the story we had cooked up in Chief Harris' office. I received some publicity; for a background slide they used a picture of me in Ram uniform. According to the commentator, I had been called in by

Glenys Christopher to return Bud to his family. That was a switch from our line, but not serious.

In the next unit a girl giggled and a man laughed. I thought of Glenys Christopher, for some reason, the composed, the competent, the long-legged Glenys Christopher. She had made a man out of Bobby but hadn't quite made a lady out of June. Could she keep Bud on the right road?

She had acted as head of the family; her parents had died when she was twenty. And now she had had her marriage annulled. When I had known her best, she had been in love with a real phony, a reading-fee agent and vanity-press author, a double phony who had lived (and died) under the name of Roger Scott. His murder had brought Glenys into my office.

It had been a strange vulnerability, her blindness about a man so obviously worthless. But he had been handsome and articulate, and perhaps his worthlessness had not been as obvious as I'd thought.

I had one shoe off and was starting to take off the other when there was a knock at my door.

I put the shoe back on and went over to answer the door.

A girl stood there in the court light, a thin girl with a tricky hairdo and brown eyes big enough to swim in. She was in basic black, a sheath, and the voice that came out of this elfin darling was deep enough for a big-bust contralto.

"Mr. Callahan?" she asked.

I nodded, trying to look into the shadows behind her, looking for a car or a man.

She must have read my glance because she said, "I came alone, Mr. Callahan. Nobody knows I'm here. My name is Mary Chavez."

"Oh, yes," I said, and hesitated. Then, "Do you want to come in?"

She nodded and came in, the sister of the dead man, the

girl identified by Skip's wife as a *very special friend*.

I closed the door and pointed to a chair near the TV. I asked, "How did you learn I was staying here?"

"Through a friend," she said; "but that isn't important. Do you know who I am?"

I nodded. She sat in the chair and I went over to sit on the bed. With her brother's body discovered only yesterday, I wondered at her composure.

She stared at the carpeting and said, "Skip didn't—didn't do—Skip was Johnny's best friend. The police in this town don't care about that. They're looking for an easy case."

"Possibly. Didn't you tell them about Johnny and Skip going up to that lodge together? I think I read that in the paper."

"I did. But now I realize they were probably both lying to me." She shook her head impatiently. "Those two—they—" She broke off, fighting her emotion.

"They lied to you often?" I prompted.

Her voice was muffled. "I'm sure they did."

"Why?"

She shook her head again and shrugged.

"Are you in love with Skip Lund?" I asked.

She looked up to face me defiantly. The brown eyes were wet. "Why do you want to know? So you can tell his wife? You're working for her, aren't you?"

"No. I'm working for Skip's son. I'm not getting paid and I don't intend to. When did Skip leave his wife?"

"About three months ago. He took an apartment downtown."

"And what did he do for a living?"

"I don't know." She took out a piece of Kleenex and wiped her eyes and nose. "But at least he stopped living on his wife's money. At least he became a *man!*"

"Didn't he ever have a business up here?"

"Not until he left her."

"And you're not sure he got one after he left her. You're not making sense, Miss Chavez."

We stared at each other and I lost, drowned in those eyes. I said softly, "I'm sure you're not lying to me. I'm sure you don't know what his business was. But did you suspect it was something illegal?"

She continued to stare at me, immovable as stone.

"I'm not out to harm him," I assured her. "I want to find him for his son. I swear to you that that is my sole interest in this case."

After what seemed like minutes but was probably only seconds, she said, "I—think I know somebody who knows what Skip's business was. I'll try to find out tomorrow morning. Do you think it might help you find him?"

"It could. This someone—is it the same person who told you I was staying here?"

Another long pause and then she nodded and stood up. "But you aren't a meddler, are you? Finding Skip—you said that was all you were interested in."

"It is. But I have to warn you. I cut a corner here and there, but I never do anything seriously illegal or withhold important information from the police. You have to understand that before you tell me anything you might regret later."

She said sadly, "I'll talk to my friend."

I went to the door with her and watched her walk out of the circle of light toward the street. A minute later I saw a pair of headlights go on out there and I closed the door again.

Active little town, this San Valdesto. Deceiving, this sleepy, self-sufficient mission town of no middle class, divided between the millionaires and the Mexicans, with no apparent class war. Apparent to *outsiders*, that is.

I fell asleep easily and dreamed of Glenys Christopher. I wakened to a world of fog.

It pressed at the windows and completely obscured the outside world, thick as country milk. All sounds were muffled; my room was like a bomb shelter.

And there was another knock at my door. One thing was sure; even trivial news traveled fast in this town—news as trivial as the address of Callahan.

It was my client, and it looked as if he had been crying.

"Ye gods!" I said. "How did you get here, Bud?"

"On my bike." He sniffed. "I found last night's paper. Mom tried to hide it from me, didn't she?"

"Come in out of that soup," I said. "Did you tell your mother you were coming way over here?"

He came in, still sniffing. I gave him a couple of tissues and said, "Blow your nose. There's nothing to cry about. Your dad hasn't been officially charged with anything." And added to myself, *Not yet*.

"They're looking for him," he said. "The police are looking for him."

"Because he was a friend of Chavez'. That doesn't mean—" And I stopped. Because I suddenly realized what else it could mean. It could mean that Skip Lund, too, might be dead.

It must have occurred to Bud at the same moment. He sat on the bed and clenched both hands tight. He was fighting tears, making a real manly effort not to be almost twelve years old.

I said, "Partner, you hang on. We're going to find your dad."

He nodded, not trusting himself to speak. He reached in under his blazer and brought out a six-by-nine photograph.

It was a lean-jawed, crew-cut young fellow, handsome

in a rural, western way, with sun-bleached eyebrows and some arrogance in the taut face.

I said, "Good-looking guy. Your dad, huh?"

He nodded. "You won't lose it, will you? It's—the only picture I have."

"I won't lose it. How did you find me, Bud?"

"I didn't go right to bed last night. I stayed up and—" He shrugged.

"And spied on us," I said. "And where does your mother think you are right now?"

His chin lifted defiantly. "In school. But I'm not going. All the kids will know about what happened. *I won't go to school!*" His voice broke and he clenched his hands again, fighting tears.

"So O.K.," I said easily. "Maybe you can stay out for a couple days. Today's Friday, anyway. But I have to phone your mother."

He nodded, not looking at me.

Glenys answered the phone. I told her, "Bud came here this morning instead of going to school. He found the newspaper. Maybe he could stay out of school, at least for today?"

"Wouldn't that be cowardly?"

A typical Glenys Christopher answer. I would never understand her, but I was forced to admire her. I said, "By your standards, possibly, Miss Christopher. By the standards of a sensitive eleven-year-old boy and a half-cowardly older private investigator, it makes complete sense to us. Have you forgotten how cruel children can be?"

"I didn't ask for a lecture," she said.

"And I'm not charging you for it. Now that we're even, would you like to drive over and pick the boy up? I imagine his bike would fit in that car you had last night. Or was that your Thursday car?"

"Oh, God! All right. I'm on the way, peasant."

That was the second time my attitude had forced her to call on the Deity. I was a good influence on the girl. I hung up and looked sternly at the boy. "I think I talked you into one day of hooky. But you'll have to go back next week. Some wise guy will probably sound off. *Belt him!*"

He stared in shock.

"Don't say 'oh, yeah' or walk away from him or try to joke out of it, understand? The first punk who opens his mouth—walk right up and *belt him.*"

He gulped and nodded uncertainly.

"And it's very likely," I said more softly, "that there will never be a second wise guy. That kind of news gets around, Bud."

"O.K.," he said. "O.K., O.K.!" He blew his nose and looked beseechingly up at me. "But how about my pop? What about him?"

"We'll know all about him when we find him," I said. I took two dimes off the dresser. "Go get us a couple of Cokes out of the machine. It's in that playroom next to the pool."

The fog was thinner now; I could almost see the units on the other side of the court. I hoped that it would clear up after breakfast, because I planned to drive up to Solvang and that was a mountain road.

ssssssssssssssss *FOUR* ssssssssssssssss

THE DEPUTY SHERIFF'S office in Solvang was in the Veterans Memorial Building. The fog was gone and it was hot up here.

Deputy Gerald Dunphy was a quiet, tall, and extremely polite man. He had just told me about finding the body of Johnny Chavez, and it had not been pleasant. Rats had eaten on Johnny for some time before he had been discovered by Deputy Dunphy.

"And he was starting to turn black," I said. "How long does that take?"

"It can vary, depending upon the temperature. They might know how long he was dead down at San Valdesto by now."

"And who identified the body?"

"His sister." He looked at some papers on his desk. "A Mary Chavez."

I imagined that sweet girl looking at the mutilated body of her brother and nausea moved through me. I must have paled.

Because Dunphy said, "Hell, two weeks ago a Cad hit a bridge abutment at a hundred miles an hour over on 101.

We pulled out what was left of four teen-agers. Johnny Chavez would have won a beauty contest up against those four."

I took a deep breath of the hot air and said nothing. I had decided not to ask him how it had happened that the city had taken over a death that had occurred in the county. Some county officers were reluctant to admit that they lacked the municipal facilities.

He glanced at a clock on the wall. "I usually have a cup of coffee about this time. Be my guest?"

"I could use it, I guess."

"And some Danish pastry?" he suggested. "The best in the state in our little town."

The pastry idea hadn't sounded interesting when it was voiced, but a cup of coffee and some fresh air helped to dispel my queasiness. And it was the best pastry I had eaten in years.

We sat in a booth in the bakery and talked about Johnny Chavez. Dunphy had been born in this area and he knew all about Johnny.

Chavez had been a phenomenal basketball player at San Valdesto High, setting scoring records that still stood. He had gone up to Cal at Berkeley because of them. But his grades hadn't kept him eligible and he had left school before the end of his freshman year.

"And then," Dunphy said wearily, "we had a former high-school hero who no longer was. But he was still Mexican, of course, and in this bigoted world that can be galling. He got into trouble, a few bar fights, a married woman whose husband had a knife . . ." Dunphy seemed to shudder. He sipped his coffee. "Two years ago he was caught selling reefers to high-school kids. That got him ninety days. First offense."

"And since?" I asked.

"Nothing on the blotter. He wasn't dumb. He was eating but not working. Your guess is as good as mine."

"Dope? Maybe he graduated from marijuana."

"It's possible. We had no reason to check him. He wasn't causing any trouble. We can't check all the people in this county who are eating but not working. We have too many like that. It's a rich county."

"But they aren't young Mexicans, are they?"

"All right, they aren't—not unless they've got a racket. Are you going to look into Johnny's possible racket?"

"I? Why should I?" I frowned. "The boy is dead. Let him rest in peace."

"Is Skip Lund dead, too?"

I continued to stare. "Not that I know of. Is he?"

"Let's start over," Dunphy said. "You're looking for Lund, aren't you? Isn't that why you stayed in town?"

"Right."

"Well, then, if Lund didn't kill his buddy, it could be reasonable to guess that he might be missing because of their little racket, whatever it was. I get the damnedest feeling that they might know more about that racket than they're willing to admit down at the S.V.P.D. This is off the record, you understand."

"Of course. I can sound out Vogel on it. He's the only officer I've had much contact with."

"Vogel," he said, and sniffed.

"You don't like him?"

"I don't. Purely personal, however. He's a highly competent police officer."

"Let's gossip," I said. "Why don't you like him?"

Dunphy finished a piece of pastry, wiped his hands carefully on a paper napkin, and lighted a cigarette.

"I'm discreet," I urged him.

He smiled uncomfortably. "All right. I'm probably class-

conscious, but he hangs around the money. He has some
mighty rich friends for a police sergeant."

"James Edward Ritter, do you mean?"

"That's one."

"Sergeant Vogel went to high school with Ritter."

"So did I."

"What's Ritter's background?"

Dunphy shrugged. "Rich kid. Mamma's boy. His father
died when Ritter was a baby. He never had to work, but
he tried a few years of insurance and served a term as mayor
down there. He's typical of the Montevista crowd, I'd say."

"You really *are* class-conscious," I kidded him. "Did that
start in high school?"

He didn't smile. He said, "I guess I was born in the wrong
county. Well, good luck, Callahan."

"Thank you. Any parting advice?"

"Better take 150," he said. "There's a lot of construction
on 101." A pause. "Oh, and you'd better drop in to see
Chief Harris when you get back to town. He'd like to talk
with you."

"Did he tell you that? How did he know I'd come here?"

Dunphy shrugged. "He phoned half an hour before you
got here. It's possible you're under observation in San Valdesto. That's off the record, too."

The fog was gone, the day was bright. Dunphy's story
of finding Johnny Chavez' body moved uneasily through
the back of my mind and I tried to concentrate on the bright
day.

Skip Lund's disappearance was beginning to show over-
tones that made me regret my promise to Bud. Johnny
Chavez had been identified by his sister as Skip's best friend
and Johnny wasn't shaping up as the local Citizen of the
Year exactly. If I found Lund, there was a possibility that
the image the boy had of his father would be destroyed.

The flivver breezed along happily; we had been traveling downhill for five miles. White smoke from all the unignited gasoline belched from her tail pipe as we slowed for the intersection at the bottom of the grade.

We were at the north edge of town now, near the motel, but I drove on toward Headquarters and Chief Chandler Harris.

He wasn't alone in his office. Sergeant Bernard Vogel was talking with him when I entered.

Harris said irritably, "Would you wait outside? The sergeant and I have some things to discuss."

I went out again, my neck hot. In the corridor two uniformed men went by and one of them said something to the other in a voice too low for me to hear. They probably weren't talking about me, but my annoyance increased.

My reputation, such as it was, had cost me money occasionally and made me some enemies worth having. No man in my trade can afford lily-white ethical standards, but no reasonable police officer who knew me considered me an outsider.

It had been painfully built, this lighter than gray reputation of mine; I had a right to resent the contempt implicit in Chief Harris' manner.

Slow, now, and easy, idiot guard, I cautioned myself. *Your temper has never earned you anything but lumps, Callahan. Be bland, be smooth, be effective.*

And don't fight City Hall. Even in the small cities. I inhaled deeply and exhaled slowly, thinking of daisies.

A mahogany-tinted man in uniform came along the corridor, smiled pleasantly at me, and walked into the chief's office. I exhaled heavily and inhaled lightly.

He came out in about a decade and a decade after that Vogel came out to tell me, "Chief Harris will see you now."

He went down the corridor as I went into the office.

Harris was reading some kind of report; he nodded to a chair without looking up.

I sat in the chair and thought grimly of lilacs.

After a year or two, he looked up and said, "Well!"

I smiled blandly.

"Been busy, haven't you?" he said.

I shrugged.

His voice was sharper. "What did Mary Chavez want?"

"First tell me why I'm under surveillance, Chief."

"We're looking for Lund. We had a hunch you might know where he is."

"It was a bad hunch."

"O.K. Now tell me what Mary Chavez wanted."

"She wanted to tell me that Lund and her brother were buddies and that Lund was no killer. She told me that she thinks now that Lund lied to her about going to the cabin with her brother."

"Oh? And how did she find out where you were?"

"I don't know. How did you?"

"That was our job. It's logical to guess she doesn't have access to the same investigative techniques. You contacted her first, didn't you?"

"No, sir."

He glared at me, his pudgy face tight, his white hair seeming to bristle.

"When I asked her how she found me, she said a friend had told her where I was. Only Mrs. Lund, her son, Miss Christopher, and Mr. Ritter were told by me where I was staying. You could question them."

"I'd rather question you. What did Dunphy tell you?"

"You ask Dunphy," I said, and stood up.

"Sit down," he said. "The Beverly Hills Department warned me about your arrogance, Callahan, but I won't take a minute of it. Now sit down!"

Our glares locked, angry as eighth-graders'. *Be bland, be smooth, be effective.* I sat down.

"What did Dunphy tell you?"

"He told me that Johnny Chavez had been eating but not working for the last couple of years. He told me he pulled four kids out of a Cad who looked worse than Chavez when he found him. He told me Solvang had the finest Danish pastry in the state, and I think he was right. That's about it, sir."

"That's *all* of it?"

"All I can remember now. If I remember more, I'll be sure to tell you. Why don't you trust me, sir?"

"I don't know you."

"You know my reputation. You checked it."

Silence.

I said quietly, "This was a county matter. How was it transferred to municipal jurisdiction?"

"Unless there's been some change recently, Mr. Callahan, we have always worked very closely with the Sheriff's Department. Did Deputy Dunphy complain about jurisdiction to you?"

"No. It was a personal question. If I'm to look for Warren Lund, I would like to do it with police co-operation. If I can't get that here in town, I'll have to work with the county."

"Do you *always* work with police co-operation?" he asked skeptically.

"Always—when I can get it. Didn't they tell you that in Beverly Hills and Los Angeles?"

Another silence.

Finally, "Are you ready to tell us now who your *real* client is in this business, Callahan?"

I said steadily, "I swear to you, sir, that my only client

is young Bud Lund, that he is not going to pay me a dime, and that I am not going to accept a dime from anyone else on this case."

He shook his head wearily. "Callahan, I wish I'd had a tape of that. Even you would realize how stupid it sounded if I could play it back."

"I won't argue with you, sir. But consider this. Miss Christopher was involved in my first case and I helped her. She is very prominent socially in Beverly Hills and her kind of people are the only kind who can afford my rates. I can use friends like Miss Christopher in Beverly Hills."

"You're making more sense now," he said grudgingly.

I had expected to. Cynical motives for cynical men. I said nothing, trying for blandness.

His voice was more restrained. "Until the recent immigration from your area, Mr. Callahan, we had an exceptionally well-policed sanctuary up here. Perhaps a part of our current problems is due only to increased population. But a few of the immigrants bear watching."

"Hoodlums?" I asked.

He shrugged. "Let's say they are people who have rather hazy connections to organized crime."

"There's no Syndicate strength in Los Angeles," I protested.

"It's bound to come. There's plenty in Vegas. Some of those newcomers were friendly with Johnny Chavez. And Lund was very close to Chavez."

"Two things come to my mind when you speak of the Syndicate—gambling and narcotics."

He nodded in agreement. "However, the—the doubtful citizens who have settled here have gone into more respectable lines, into real-estate speculation and small businesses, businesses too small to support their style of living."

A uniformed man came in, put some papers on his desk, and went out.

I said, "Do you have the address of Lund's apartment?"

He nodded. "Why?"

"If he's around, he might try to sneak back for some clothes or something."

He rummaged through some papers and found the address. I put it down in my notebook. He said, "Chavez was shot with a .30-.30 rifle from a distance. He'd been dead for about three days when Dunphy found him. The second I learn you are keeping even the tiniest scrap of information from this Department you'll be in extremely hot water. Good afternoon."

Police co-operation, San Valdesto variety.

"Thank you, sir," I said smoothly and blandly, and went out to the friendlier world beyond his door.

So, a small-town man who was getting big-town problems and undoubtedly knew he wouldn't be a match for them. I was only one target for his burning sense of inferiority; there were probably others.

I went out to the hot flivver and pointed it toward Montevista.

My client's Aunt Glenys was out in the yard, digging up some bulbs for one of the flower beds near the house. She was wearing shorts, and lust moved through me lazily. She was not the kind who usually moved me; it must have been her unattainable composure that acted as a challenge.

She stood up as I parked the car. She pulled off her heavy work gloves and came over.

"Bud around?" I asked.

She shook her head. "He went to school."

"Your idea?" I asked accusingly.

"No. His. And he said he was going to *belt* the first kid

who opened his *yap.*'' The accusation was in her voice now. "And I wonder whose idea *that* was?"

"I don't know, but it's a good one. Let's not fight, Glenys. It's too damned hot. And you're too damned pretty."

"Thank you. Is Miss Bonnet coming up for the weekend?"

I smiled slyly. "Not if you don't want her to. I can still stall her if you have any—"

"Oh, shut up!" she said. "You're so obsessively vulgar. What *is* it? What's *wrong* with you?"

"I'm a product of a sick society," I explained. "Is there any of that High Life around?"

And now there was a crack in her composure and a faint flush in her tanned cheeks. "I—ah—remembered. I had a case of Einlicher delivered this morning."

I stared, wallowing in her blush. This girl. . . . If I weren't such a lout, with a lout's approach, I'd bet. . . .

"What are you smirking about?" she asked me sharply. "What's on your vulgar mind?"

"You. You're so gracious, so disciplined. You did such a fine job on Bobby. Your taste is flawless, your hair is—"

"Oh, shut up!" she said, but less angrily. "Would you like your beer out here?"

I nodded, and she pointed. "Go around to that side of the house. It's cooler over there."

I went the way she had indicated and she went into the house. I settled in a weather-stained rattan chair under a jacaranda tree and tried to think of comforting words for my client, who should be home from school soon.

Then Glenys was coming across the dry grass with a bottle of Einlicher for each of us, and I began to feel less disturbed. That Einlicher, it won't solve your problems, but it will put them into easier focus.

"Anything?" she asked me. She took a chair near mine.

"Nothing. I have a very fragile permission from Chief Harris to continue without getting the gas chamber. I have a feeling his blessing might be revoked any second."

"June could have Jim put in a word for you," she said. "Jim was mayor here for one term."

"I know. But James Edward Ritter is not likely to want Skip found, is he?"

"What do you mean? That was rotten, Brock."

"I withdraw the statement. Isn't he in love with June?"

No answer.

"And isn't June in love with Skip?"

"I certainly hope she isn't. I—"

She broke off as Bud came around the corner of the house. He had a scraped bruise under one eye. "Well?" he asked.

"No luck today, partner. What happened to your eye?"

He looked at his Aunt Glenys and down at the dry grass.

"How about the second wise guy?" I asked. "Was there one?"

He shook his head. "You were right." He took a breath. "Could I go with you tomorrow when you look some more?"

"Sorry. I always work alone."

He looked at the glass in my hand. "I didn't know you drank, too."

"Only beer," I said. "I don't smoke."

Nothing from him.

I said, "The Dodgers won today."

"I know." He took another breath. "Brock—do you think that—I mean, you think he's all right? Maybe—" He broke off, his chin quivering.

"I don't know anything yet, Bud," I said gently. "I won't know anything until I find him."

"But you're going to keep looking, huh?"

"Absolutely."

His mother called him then, and he went off with a wave.

When he was out of the range of our voices, Glenys said, "Send the bill to me, Brock."

I shook my head stubbornly. "Nope. This one has to be on the house."

"You're a strange man," she said.

"And proud to be," I assured her.

FIVE

I ATE DINNER at a downtown restaurant. The local paper I had bought gave me no information on the death of Chavez that I didn't have and gave only last-line notice to the report that Lund was still being sought by the police.

If I was still under Department surveillance, my half-trained eyes could not observe it. There was no human resembling a cop in the restaurant and I hadn't been followed from Montevista, I was almost sure.

Of course, I hadn't known I'd been watched before until the chief had admitted it. My mind went back over the day. What had I accomplished for my client? Nothing. Perhaps if Mary Chavez learned what Skip's "business" was, as she was going to try to do today, it would be a stronger lead than I'd had so far.

Unless he was beyond newspaper, radio, and TV communication, he *had* to know that he was wanted. And if he knew but didn't reveal himself, what could that mean? If it meant what it seemed to mean, I was doing Bud no favor.

At the motel, there had been a long-distance call for me,

47

according to the note under my door. I phoned the operator's number.

It was Jan who had phoned. She said, "I can't make it, Brock, damn it! The Kesselrings *insist* I spend the weekend up at their ranch."

"To hell with the Kesselrings," I said. "They bought your time and talent, not your soul, lady."

"Brock, this is the biggest commission I've lined up in a year. You simply don't say no to people like the Kesselrings." A pause. "Only an economic *idiot* would refuse the Kesselrings."

Personal, she was getting. I said, "Or a person of integrity. Just remember this—I wanted you here. The decision not to come was made by you, out of greed."

"Oh?" Her voice was an arctic wind, cooling an iceberg. "Are you threatening me with something? Something like adultery, perhaps? Some aging bar girl, maybe, has succumbed to your porcine charms?"

"Try not to be vulgar," I said. "Good night, moneybags." I hung up.

Outside, it was dark now. Car doors slammed and toilets growled and TV eyes went sock, sock, sock, bang, bang, bang. I sat their sulking, missing my girl. We would never be married—*never*.

The ring of the phone startled me.

The voice was feminine and deep, and because of the faint accent I thought for a moment it was Mary Chavez.

But she identified herself as Juanita Rico. She said, "I have a place called Chickie's at the other end of town from where you are. Could you drop in and talk with me tonight?"

"I could. Are you the friend of Mary Chavez?"

"I'm one of her friends. She has *many*. You might mention that to Sergeant Vogel next time you're together."

"Did Vogel mistreat Mary?"

"Not physically. He was rude and insulting."

"I see. Chickie's, eh? What's the address, Miss Rico?"

She gave me the address and told me it was *Mrs.* not *Miss* and said she would be there all evening.

I had lamented a wasted day, but it wouldn't be over until midnight and perhaps it would still bear fruit.

It was in the Mexican district, a long stucco building with two steps leading up to the double front door. In the window a red neon sign identified it as *Chickie's*.

There was only one other customer this early in the evening. He stood at the far end of the battered bar, a lanky, redheaded man in jeans and sport shirt. In a far corner a thin-faced Mexican with bony fingers played a soft and melancholy guitar.

The woman behind the bar was olive-skinned with a strong face and full-bodied figure, though not in any sense fat. She was a shade on the buxom side for my taste but plainly *all woman*.

"Mr. Callahan?" she asked.

I nodded.

"I'm Juanita Rico."

"How do you do, Juanita. And who is Chickie?"

She frowned. "The man who used to own this place. Why?"

"Just wondered."

A pause. "Drink?" She glanced meaningly toward the man at the end of the bar. "We will talk later. It won't be long."

"O.K. Beer. Draught beer if you have it. Otherwise a bottle of High Life."

She poured a glass from a spigot and set it in front of me. I sipped it slowly, listening to the melodic lamentations of the guitar. In a few minutes the redhead finished his drink, wiped his mouth with the back of his hand, and went out without a good night.

Juanita Rico made a face. "He never says a word, that one. He walks in, orders two double bourbons, drinks them, walks out. Maybe he don't like us, huh?"

"Maybe he's a mute," I suggested. "What about Skip Lund, Mrs. Rico?"

She ignored the question. "He's no mute. He's got a voice when he orders." She made another face. "Angloes! Phooey!"

"I'm one," I said. "What about Skip Lund?"

The sound of the guitar stopped. I turned to meet the stare of the lanky man with the thin face. He stared back without animosity or interest.

Juanita said something to him in Spanish and he began to play again.

"If I tell you about Skip," she said, "you will have to tell the police, no?"

"It depends upon what you tell me. My interest is his son, but I can't work in opposition to the police."

"My interest is his son, too," she said sadly. "That is why I phoned you." She sighed. "Skip is a nice boy; he could be a better father."

"And husband," I added.

She made a face again. "Phooey! Who can be a good husband in Montevista?"

"Skip's alive, then?" I asked.

She nodded. "I'm sure he is."

"You don't *know?*"

"If a man is out of sight, how can you know he's alive? The manager of your motel, do you *know* he's alive right now?"

"You're quibbling," I said. "And Johnny Chavez? What did Lund have to do with that?"

"Nothing. He was not with Johnny when he died."

"Mrs. Rico," I said gravely, "if you can prove that, your duty is to tell it to the police."

"There are reasons why I cannot. And if you tell them I said that, I will call you a liar and bring witnesses to fix you *good* in this town."

I stared at her.

She smiled. "You are not the police. You are working for the boy. I will see that Skip contacts the boy."

"And what good will that do," I protested, "if he's still on the wrong side of the law?"

Her brown eyes flashed and her full body was rigid. "Can you prove that Skip Lund is on the wrong side of the law?"

"Not right now. His buddy had a record."

"Skip has no record."

The guitar stopped again. I gave him my attention once more and he returned the favor.

I looked back at Juanita. "What is he, the suspense orchestrator or something?"

"He came to the end of the piece," she said calmly. "He stops before he starts another. Are you nervous, Mr. Callahan?"

I said, "I came here in good faith for a charity client. I wasn't received in good faith."

"How can you be? Haven't you admitted you must work with the police?"

"And you don't?"

"Have another beer," she said, "on the house." She took my glass and poured another.

"And you don't?" I repeated.

"What business is that of yours?"

"It puts Lund in a bad light if you don't."

She exhaled heavily and stared at me in anger. "Mr. Callahan, though you are a stranger here, I offered you perhaps the first help you have been offered in this town. And you immediately make noises like a cop. In this place, *we do not like cops*. Does that put us on the wrong side of the law?''

"Generally, yes."

"Good night to you," she said. "Drink up and go. To hell with you."

I thought of my client, waiting for a word, any word. I thought of the unreasonable Chief Chandler Harris and the belligerent Sergeant Bernard Vogel and the only man who had smiled at me down at Headquarters, the Mexican patrolman.

I said humbly, "Believe me, my only interest in this case is to find the father of my eleven-year-old client. Where did I go wrong with you?"

"Drink," she said, "and go. I should have realized when you informed the police Mary came to see you last night that you could not be trusted."

"I swear to you, Juanita, that the police found that out by themselves. They have had me watched here ever since I brought Bud back to his mother."

Her eyes widened. She went to the window and looked out. She said something in Spanish to the guitar player and he carefully laid down his instrument and went through the swinging door that probably led to the kitchen.

She came back to ask, "Do you think they followed you here?"

"I doubt it. I couldn't see anybody. But I didn't see the man when they were watching me."

"Perhaps, then," she suggested, "you are not such a great friend of the police?"

I said evenly, "I can't fight them and stay in business. But I am a better friend of young Warren Lund."

She stared at me as though she was reading more into

my statement than I had intended. Then she said, "Callahan, there are moral acts which are illegal and legal acts which are very immoral. Can you believe that?"

"Is it a riddle? I'm not good at riddles."

"Isn't that your business, riddles?"

I smiled at her. "I suppose. I am not very good at my business. I am only strong and stubborn."

"You have a nice smile," she said. "You don't look anything like a cop when you smile."

"Let's see your smile," I said.

She took my glass and refilled it. She smiled. "Some enchiladas, perhaps? I make the best enchiladas in town."

"Not now," I said. "Maybe later."

There was no point in crowding her. She was a strong personality and this was *mañana* land. And where else did I have to go?

The guitar player, who had gone out through the kitchen, came in again through the front door and spoke softly to her in Spanish. She nodded and he went back to the guitar.

"All clear?" I asked.

"Yes."

I sipped my beer. "That Mary Chavez is a sweet girl, isn't she?"

"An angel. They will be married, she and Skip. He is already taking instructions from the priest."

"From the priest? When I was a Catholic, Juanita, divorced people could not be married by a priest."

"You were a dumb Catholic, Callahan. If the parties were originally married outside the Church, they are not married in the eyes of the Church. Skip was not married before to a Catholic.

She was wrong, I felt sure. But it was not a time to argue religion. Nor was I qualified. And though the love life of Skip Lund was none of my business and Mary Chavez was a sweet girl, and though I was sure that Lund had sound reasons, I was sad.

Because Bud, like all boys, needed a father, a father of his own blood.

The door opened and the redhead was back.

Mrs. Rico stared at him and then at me. This was obviously a change in the man's routine, and it had startled her.

He didn't go to the end of the bar. He came over to stand next to me and say gruffly, "Double bourbon."

"I know," she said. "I ought to by now, huh?"

He nodded without looking at her.

She poured it and went over to talk with the guitar player.

The redhead said quietly, "I usually get out of here before all those spics come in. But I figured if you can take it, I can."

"If you're bigoted," I said, "why come in here at all?"

"Bigoted? What's that? That mean you don't like Mexicans?"

"That's one of the things it means. Nobody's forcing you to come in here."

He studied me doubtfully. He had a big, ugly, freckled face and faded-blue eyes. I could guess he had been in a few bar fights in his time and won his share.

"A wise guy?" he asked ominously.

"No. Only puzzled. Is the whisky better here? Or maybe cheaper?"

His smile was cynical. "Why are you here?"

"On business. Why else?"

Juanita was back behind the bar now and Red's eyes moved slyly that way and I got his message. There was lust in the slyness, a mute, aching lust.

Juanita began to wash some glasses.

I said quietly to the redhead, "She's married and she doesn't like angloes. It's hopeless, Red."

"Married, huh? Where'd you hear that?"

"It's *Mrs*. Rico, isn't it?"

"That don't mean she's married *now*. I been in here plenty and I never saw no husband around."

Some more people came in and Juanita moved down the bar to serve them. The guitar moved into more cheerful melodies to match the cheerful patrons, laboring men and their perfumed wives trying to ignore tomorrow.

In one corner a young couple danced, close and well and oblivious. Juanita watched them smilingly.

"Think she'd like to dance?" the redhead asked me.

I shrugged.

"Whyn't you ask her?" he suggested. "And then I can cut in."

I shook my head.

He grumbled something I couldn't understand and called to Juanita, "Another double here."

She came down to pour it. She stood in front of us and poured his drink and then ignored him, asking me, "Happy people, aren't they? Not like Montevista."

Was she putting in a word for Mary Chavez, a word against June Lund? I smiled, not committing myself.

Red said hoarsely, "Could I buy you a drink, Juanita?"

"Why not?" she said, and looked at him without interest. She poured a shot and held it high. "Your health, Mr. — ?"

"Hovde," he said shakily. "Lars Hovde. My friends call me Red."

"Your health, Mr. Hovde," she said, and downed her drink in one swallow. She smiled at me and went to the other end of the bar again.

"Hard to get, huh?" Red scoffed. "She don't fool me."

"Patience, Red," I said. "Be smooth."

"Sure." He looked down at his faded jeans and fingered the wet spot on his cheap sport shirt. "I got better clothes than this, but I didn't want her to think I was too fancy.

They don't like that, when you're fancy."

"*Women* don't like it when you're fancy?"

"Not spics," he said.

His bigotry was annoying enough. But the way he was hoisting the doubles he was bound to get louder. And this was no place to use that ugly word loud enough to be heard.

I walked up to where Juanita stood and told her, "This redhead is beginning to annoy me. I could belt him, but we don't want any cops, do we?"

"I could tell him to leave," she suggested.

"No. I'll go. And about Lund . . . ?"

"I'll phone you tomorrow, if I decide to take the chance," she said. "I couldn't help you tonight anyway. I don't know exactly where he is tonight."

"I don't know where I'll be tomorrow," I said. "I'd better call you."

"Any time after noon," she said. "*Amigo,* you may tell the boy his father is no killer and he will hear from him."

"Has he been away?" I asked. "On a trip?"

"Your nose is long. Tell the boy what I told you."

I went out without saying good night to Lars Hovde. The night was cold and clear after the hot day and I stood for a few seconds, breathing it in.

Behind me, the laughter of the happy people—and I hoped Hovde wouldn't change the mood in there with his loser's hatreds.

I climbed into the flivver hating the big, dumb bastard. Motel rooms are lonely. Friday night was a bad night for TV and I didn't even like the good nights. That had been a warm and friendly bar, and who knows what might have developed, either revelatory or romantic, as the guitar and the alcohol worked their blend of magic?

The flivver hummed along, oblivious to my sense of frustration.

And then, as I turned into the drive behind my unit, another car turned in ahead of me and continued toward the rear. It was a big car, a black Continental, and a ghost of this afternoon's transient lust came back to haunt me.

Maybe that bastard Hovde had done me a favor; it looked like Glenys Christopher's car.

SIX

THE CONTINENTAL PULLED into the stall directly behind my room; I pulled into the stall on its left. The light over the rear door was bright enough to show me that it was Glenys behind the wheel. She looked my way and stepped out of the car.

"Hello," I said.

"Hello. Where have you been? I called twice."

"I've been working."

"Oh? Then Jan isn't here?"

Did you really think she was? I thought. I shook my head.

"Any news about Warren?" she asked, after a second.

"Some hope. I think I've met someone who knows where he is."

"Someone named Mary Chavez?"

I shook my head again. "I'll know more tomorrow. Would you like to come in or is that a vulgar question?"

She stared at the ground. She might have blushed, but I couldn't tell in this light. She said softly, "Bud's staying with a friend and my sister went out with Jim someplace. I—was bored."

It didn't figure. Not Glenys Christopher. Not that inhibited, reserved, and disciplined lady. I couldn't think of anything unvulgar to say.

She seemed to be holding her breath, and her voice was tight. "I—uh—brought some Einlicher."

"Wonderful," I said. "We'll have a quiet bottle and talk about the old days."

She seemed to be appraising me and I think there was a moment when she was ready to get back into the car. But finally she said, "It's on the floor in front."

It was a canvas cooler and it took both my hands to carry it. I gave her my key and she opened the door. After she had turned on the light, she asked, "What time will Jan be here?"

"She isn't coming," I said. "She has to spend the weekend with a client. Money, money, money, that's Jan."

She was sitting next to the TV when I came back from the kitchenette with our beer. She sighed and said, "That's not a happy house over in Montevista. I had to get out of it."

Sure, sure, sure. . . . I handed her the beer and asked, "Was it a happy house before Skip left it?"

"For a while."

"Glenys," I asked gently, "did you try to make Skip Lund over into something he wasn't?"

"I? Now what did *that* mean?"

"Well," I explained, "one of the things he wasn't was Warren Temple Lund the Second."

Her face tightened. She didn't comment.

I smiled. "O.K., tell me off. It's none of my damned business."

Her chin lifted and she said coolly, "I didn't try to make Skip Lund into something he wasn't. Perhaps if I had, the police wouldn't be looking for him now."

"O.K. Your point. Let's not fight."

"Why not? You're losing."

I laughed and she smiled. And then I asked, "How long were you married?"

"Two months. It was never legal. He had . . . neglected to divorce one of his previous wives."

"Anyone I know?"

She shook her head, her eyes reminiscent. "I . . . went into that marriage a virgin. At *twenty-eight.*"

Well. . . . What in hell do you say to that kind of frankness?

She looked at me candidly. "Did I embarrass you?"

"A little. Would you like more beer?"

"I guess. Does my being here embarrass you?"

"Nope. Why should it? We're friends, in a way." I went to get more beer. My hands shook as I poured it.

When we were settled again, she said, "I was a sadly innocent girl who had been deluding herself for years that she was self-sufficient. The man was—nothing, just as Roger Scott was. But he taught me that even a nothing man is better than a women's club luncheon."

Glenys Christopher letting down her hair; it was beyond belief.

I said, "You are beautiful and intelligent and desirable. You are single only by choice."

"Huh!" she said. "Only a man could believe that." The glass in her hand was unsteady for a second and she changed the subject. "To get back to Skip Lund—neither June nor I tried to make him over. He came up here without any thought of going into business. He spent forty thousand dollars for that damned boat and practically *lived* on it. June can't stand the water."

"Boat?" I said blankly. Something flickered in my unconscious mind, one fact trying to relate to another. "Boat?" I said again, trying to trigger the pattern.

She shook her head bitterly. "It was a new kind of hot rod for Skip Lund. He'll always be a hot-rodder."

I asked, "Where did he get the money?"

She said dully, "From June. Where else? Have you been briefed on the police history of his good friend, Johnny Chavez?"

"Yes." I thought of the reefers. Narcotics and a boat; the flicker had more substance now. Narcotics and a boat and Juanita saying she didn't know *exactly* where Skip was right now. *Exactly* had been a strange word, but not for a man at sea.

"What are you thinking about?" Glenys asked.

"A theory. A hunch. Was Skip's boat seaworthy enough to make Mexico?"

"I have no idea. Why? Do you think he might have gone there?"

"It was just a random thought, a hunch from left field. Your glass is empty."

"Fill it," she said.

I brought in a bottle and filled her glass. As I was pouring, she said, "I worry about Bud."

"Of course. But he's not your responsibility, Glenys. Bobby and June might have been, but Bud isn't."

Her fine face lifted and her eyes mocked me. "Is he yours? You won't even accept pay for helping him."

"I'm sentimental," I explained.

The chin lifted again, but not defiantly. Beseechingly. "And I'm not?"

Vulnerable, that strong and beautiful face, beseeching.

I bent and kissed her.

For less than a second there was resistance in her soft lips, and then they answered me. I straightened to look down and see some mist in her eyes.

Her voice was hoarse and husky. "I suppose we're heading

somewhere we shouldn't. Will you promise to consider it therapeutic for me?" She put a hand on my forearm. "And *never, never* mention it again?"

It would be indelicate to go into the clinical details of what followed, but it required a lot of patience on my part. Her morality was strong and extended to sex because of the twenty-eight barren years. Though her need was great (the annulment was three years back), she was too basically and instinctively a lady to enjoy the bed fully without proper conditioning.

Patiently, slowly, gently, and cunningly, the vulgar Callahan worked toward the deeper breath and the first indicative and anticipatory quiver.

Slowly but successfully, until the body writhed and the whimpers no longer were protesting and a great, soaring catharsis was achieved.

She shuddered, she sighed, she stretched. And asked sadly, "Will I ever be able to look at Jan again?"

"You don't see her much, do you?"

"Lately I have. I'm thinking of redoing the house."

"Glenys," I said sternly, "get married. Find a man you can trust, one with more money than you have, and let him buy you a house. Damn it, you always get involved with con men!"

"Always? Twice."

"That was always for you. Would you like another beer?"

She laughed quietly. "Heavens, what a hedonist you are! Tell me, is it a happy philosophy, Callahan?"

"It serves." I put on a robe and sat on the edge of the bed. "Glenys, get married before you turn to stone. You're wasting yourself and depriving some solid citizen of a first-class wife."

She sat up and put a tender hand on my cheek. "Old Uncle Brock! Who needs a cow when milk is free?"

"Don't be vulgar," I said. "That's my pitch. You can't be the mother to the whole damned world, Glenys."

"I'll be the girl friend, then," she said lightly. "Will you be in touch with Skip tomorrow?"

"I hope to be."

"And then you'll be going home?"

"I suppose. Maybe I'll wait until Sunday."

"Could we—have dinner or something tomorrow? You're nice to be with, when you try to be."

"I'll phone you in the morning," I promised. "Drive carefully, now."

The big black car went away and I sat on the edge of the bed, a robe over my nakedness, finishing the bottle of beer. Glenys had left by the back door. When someone knocked on the front, I thought perhaps she had come back that way.

It wasn't Glenys; it was the thin girl with the rich voice and big eyes, Mary Chavez.

She looked at my robe and up at me embarrassedly. "I'm sorry. I heard voices before and knew you had company. I heard the car leave and thought . . . I mean . . ."

"Come in," I said. "Don't stand in the light."

She hesitated—and came in. I closed the door.

She stood next to the doorway, her gaze carefully staying above my shoulders. "Did Juanita tell you anything?"

"As little as possible. She's a cautious woman. She thinks she can get in touch with Skip tomorrow."

"I see." She licked her lower lip. "Did she say where Skip had been?"

"She didn't. Do you know?"

She shook her head. "Do you think—I mean, there's something dishonest going on, isn't there?"

"A reasonable man would have to think so. I'm surprised you don't know more than you do," I said.

She looked startled. "Why should I?"

I didn't answer.

But she must have read my mind. Because she said, "I can guess why you said that. We are burying him tomorrow. Until he went up to Berkeley, he was a good boy." Her chin quivered and she glared at me. "It's an anglo world. You don't know about people like us."

"I know about soft and innocent girls like you," I said. "You were born to be suckered. Get smart now, Mary, before it's too late. Skip Lund is shaping up as more of a bum every minute."

She said fiercely, "That's not true. In Beverly Hills he had a good business. And he'll have one here when he has a wife who doesn't need diamonds and sable and European vacations. He's a fine, straight man!"

"He's a hot-rodder who married money," I said.

Wham!

What a right hand. . . . It hadn't been a slap. It had been a fist, smack on my mouth, and blood ran down from my torn lower lip and I stared at her in untainted admiration.

She began to cry.

I had thought her soft, but in her neighborhood she couldn't be soft and grow to her age looking as *she* did. She might not be soft, but I would lay odds she was pure.

"Your knuckle's bleeding," I said. "You'd better wash it."

She shook her head, still crying.

I went into the bathroom and soaked a washcloth with soapy water.

I brought it out to her and said, "Please wash that hand. I apologize if I said something wrong. Would I have said it if I wasn't worried about you?"

She sniffed and took the washcloth and went into the bathroom. I sat on the bed with a piece of Kleenex, wiping the blood from my lip.

When she came out again, she was no longer crying. I

grinned at her. "Juanita called you an angel, but that was quite a right you threw. Where did you learn that?"

"Where I live. From Johnny. I shouldn't have hit you. May I wash it for you?"

"It's nothing. Juanita told me Vogel gave you a bad time. Why?"

"Because I told him I would not sign a statement that Skip went to the shack with my brother."

"Didn't Skip tell you he was going with Johnny?"

She stared at me, her lips compressed.

"O.K., Mary. So you play it your way. If I said anything wrong, I'm sorry. Fight City Hall, marry a man who can't settle down, hate angloes. Good night!"

"You're angry," she said softly. "You have a right to be. Good night."

She went out and I went to the refrigerator to get an ice cube for my swelling lip. Uncle Brock . . . I had given Glenys quite a lecture for having the same faults I had. Uncle Brock. . . . To hell with all of them, and particularly the lambs.

The girl might be vulnerable, but her friends were not. I went to bed and tried to forget them all.

The morning dawned clear and bright. This was a beautiful town. With Jan gone from Beverly Hills, I might as well stay until Sunday and write it off as vacation. If Juanita came through, my mission would be completed today. Tomorrow I could use the pool and maybe even take Glenys to dinner.

And if Juanita didn't come through . . . ?

She wouldn't be available until this afternoon; I could use the morning for my own research. But, first, some pancakes; there was a restaurant down the road that sold nothing else but all the kinds of pancakes there were.

A double order of French pancakes with boysenberry

syrup and whipped butter, fried eggs, and little pork sausages—I was halfway into this delicate repast when Sergeant Bernard Vogel walked in.

He stood just inside the doorway, giving us all the eye, and I had the uncomfortable feeling that he hadn't come in to eat.

When he spotted me, he came over. "Saw your car outside. Missed you at the motel. A few questions, if you don't mind."

"What good would it do to mind? Sit down, Sergeant."

He sat down across from me and shook his head to the waitress who came over. He watched me carefully as he said, "Friend of yours got clobbered last night. Man named Lars Hovde."

"He's no friend of mine," I said. "That's why I came home early. He was heading for trouble, last I saw him."

"Where was this?"

I looked at him levelly. "What did Hovde tell you?"

"He said it was a place called Chickie's."

"He told the truth."

"And what were you doing there?"

"Having a beer. What happened to Hovde?"

"He was slugged a couple minutes after he left the place." Vogel paused. "And knifed. He's over at St. Mary's Hospital right now."

I said easily, "That's a tough neighborhood. And Red's got some unfortunate attitudes. Last night was the first time I ever saw the man and I hope it's the last."

Vogel's face was grim and his voice deadly. "Let's start over. What were you doing at Chickie's?"

I finished the last half of my final sausage and slowly stirred a spoonful of sugar into my coffee. I said, "Sergeant, I have to respect some confidences if I'm to work effectively. The way it looks right now, I'll be through here this afternoon. I'll come in and see you then. Fair enough?"

He shook his head.

"It's the way I work," I told him.

He shook his head again. "Not in this town."

I kept the anger from my voice. "Your boss checked me and I checked out. I'm not one of those crummy divorce peepers, Sergeant."

He studied me as though I were a bug. He was getting to me with his quiet contempt.

He stood up. "All right, you came in crying for co-operation and we were suckered. You ask another citizen of this town a single question and we'll run you in and *really* sweat you. You got it?"

"Could I speak with the chief about that? You're being unreasonable, Sergeant."

"You've had your chance," he said harshly. "We'll be watching you again, Callahan."

His voice had risen and customers at other tables glanced our way and a few of them stopped eating to stare.

Anger and embarrassment surged in me. Only his badge was keeping him vertical and conscious. I stared at my coffee, ignoring him.

When I looked up again, he was gone.

The other customers were avoiding my glance; when I went to pay the cashier, she took my money and murmured a "thank you" while she carefully kept her eyes every place but on mine.

I went back to the motel, for lack of any better place to go. I was burning at Vogel's officious and arrogant stupidity, but I wasn't quite angry enough to disregard his warning.

I called the Lund home and asked for Glenys. I asked her, "Have you said anything to Bud about the possibility of his father's being found today?"

"No. I thought I'd wait until I had something more definite from you."

"You might not get anything more definite from me. Sergeant Vogel just told me to keep my nose out of the case."

"Why would he do that? What happened?"

"He doesn't think I'm working with the Department. He doesn't understand my position."

A silence, and then, "I'll have June talk with Jim. Jim is not only a friend of Vogel's; he knows Chief Harris very well."

"O.K. You phone as soon as you get a clearance for me."

"It might take some time," she said. "Jim's playing golf this morning." A pause. "Why don't you do what needs to be done and I'll start working at this end?"

"All right," I said. "Fine."

I should have stayed with my original hunch. James Edward Ritter was not likely to come to the aid of anyone searching for Skip Lund. Ritter would prefer to have Skip missing forever.

⪼⪼⪼ *SEVEN* ⪼⪼⪼

THE WHARF WAS an extension of the town's main street and the flivver rattled over the wooden roadway at the legal five miles an hour. The Pacific had some blue in it again today; clouds hovered over the Channel Islands. Boats of all shapes and sizes bobbed in the light swell of the harbor.

I drove past the rambling sea-food restaurant and parked in a three-car space near a lunch stand. The morning's pancakes were not digested yet, but I could always use a cup of coffee.

It was a four-stool stand, open on two sides. The man behind the counter was thin and tanned, wearing blue cotton trousers and a T Shirt.

I climbed onto a stool and said, "Just coffee. Black."

He smiled, poured it, and set it on the counter.

"Quite a boat town, isn't it?" I commented.

"Boats and horses," he admitted. "You from down south?"

Los Angeles, he meant. That's what they called it here. I nodded.

"How's the smog?" he asked.

"Getting worse. How much boat could a man buy for forty thousand dollars?"

He yawned and scratched himself. "I suppose it would depend on how sharp he was at dickering. Some guys figure a thousand dollars a foot, but I could sure as hell do a lot better than *that*."

"Could a forty-thousand-dollar boat make Mexico?"

"Hell, yes." Then his eyes narrowed and he looked at me doubtfully. I thought I saw recognition there. He asked quietly, "Why do you want to know?"

I shrugged. "A friend of mine bought one. I was just wondering."

His face was blank. "This friend got a name?"

"Warren Temple Lund the Second," I said.

"Skip," he said quietly. "You're a cop, huh? I should have known, the size of you."

"A private investigator," I said, "working for Skip's son. I'm not getting paid and I can keep a secret if it doesn't violate the law."

He nodded. "I know you now. I thought your face was familiar." He extended a hand. "The great Callahan. Man, what's happened to those Rams?"

"They're rebuilding," I explained. "How well do you know Skip?"

"Well enough to like him. Most of the gang down here do. He might not be so popular in Montevista, but he's *our* kind of people."

"Do you know where he is?"

He looked out at the boats in the yacht basin and back at me. He shook his head.

"His boat there?"

He paused, and nodded. "Chavez is probably aboard right now."

I stared at him. "Chavez? He's dead."

"*Pete* Chavez," he explained. "Johnny's cousin." He looked thoughtfully at his image in the glistening coffee urn. "Maybe I got too much mouth, huh? I don't even know you—only your rep."

"Up here the police don't even know that. At least they don't respect it." I sipped my coffee and kept my voice casual. "When did the boat come in?"

He studied me for seconds and then said doubtfully, "This morning, around eight. Don't quote me."

"I promise I won't. Think Skip is aboard now?"

The thin man's smile was cynical. "With the law looking for him? He's not that simple."

"Is he outside the law? What does he have to fear from the law?"

His voice was harsh. "In this town the law didn't like Johnny Chavez or his friends or his relatives. Skip and Johnny were buddies. And you know who else is buddies— Sergeant Vogel and ex-Mayor James Blowhard Ritter, that puke! That's some deal for Skip Lund, isn't it? What chance has the man got?"

I said nothing.

"And," he went on, "with Ritter lusting for Skip's wife, you want Skip to turn himself in?"

I stared at him wonderingly. "Where did you learn all that?"

"A town this size," he said contemptuously, "what else we got to talk about?"

"And you admire Skip Lund?"

He looked at me evenly. "Why not?"

I shrugged. "The picture I've been getting hasn't been so—well, favorable."

"Maybe you got one side of it, the Montevista side. You might get a better picture if you asked about Skip around here."

I thought of Mary Chavez' telling me about Skip and Johnny and how they had lied to her and a hunch came to me.

I said to the counterman, "So Skip Lund and Johnny's cousin were out of town when Johnny Chavez was killed?"

He frowned, staring. "I didn't say that."

His face was guarded; he was probably beginning to regret some of the things he had told me. I was no longer the great Callahan to him. Small-town insularity had built a wall between us.

"Is Skip's boat visible from here?" I asked him.

He said nothing.

"I can find out," I told him. I put a coin on the counter and slid off the stool.

He hesitated and then turned toward the harbor. "That fifty-footer with the brown hull and white cabin." He pointed and turned to face me. "If Pete Chavez is aboard, don't get lippy. He's not tall, but he's awful damned tough."

"I'll be careful," I said. "Thank you."

The flivver went rumbling back across the planks once more, toward the shore. Water beneath us and on both sides of us, the ancient pier weatherworn but solid.

I had a pattern in my mind now. By hint and by hunch a pattern had taken shape. If one believed in Skip Lund's innocence, there had to be a reason why he hadn't reported to the police. I was sure that Lund knew that he couldn't be railroaded if his alibi was sound. Justice was dispensed by judges, not policemen.

So there had to be another reason why he was missing. Perhaps he had been on a trip, an ocean trip. Or perhaps his alibi would put him in water almost as hot as suspicion of murder. Either of these things could be true, and maybe both.

At the end of the pier a squad car pulled up alongside and I waited for a signal from the man next to the driver.

But he was looking straight ahead, ignoring me.

I let them slide by before making a left turn and starting to breathe again.

There was a parking lot here that served the yacht club and the dock area; I pulled in and found a space near the water. The pier that led to the slip holding the fifty-footer wasn't far away.

Both the brown hull and the white cabin looked newly painted; there was a man aboard, squatting on the deck, his back to me. He appeared to be wiping up something that had spilled. He was a short man with stocky legs and enormous shoulders.

From the pier, I called, "Pete Chavez?"

He turned without rising. "That's my name. And what's yours?" He had a strong-featured, walnut-brown face, now scowling.

"My name is Callahan," I said. "I'm looking for Skip Lund."

He stood up, appraising me. "He's not here. What's your beef?"

"No beef. Pure charity. I promised his son I'd find him. His son is a friend of mine."

"He's not here," he said again. "So long."

I kept my voice friendly. "If you know where he is, would you just ask him to phone his boy?"

"No," he said.

I stared at him; he grinned at me. There was no warmth in his grin.

My hands trembled, but my voice was calm. "O.K. Play it your way. So long." I turned to leave.

"You're not fooling me," he said. "You cheap peeper."

This had been a frustrated search, too full of ill-mannered people. I turned and studied him contemptuously from head to foot.

"Don't let your size give you any foolish ideas, big boy," he said, still grinning. "Go while you're still able to walk."

"Shorty," I explained patiently, "I came on a mission of mercy. I have no beef with you or with Lund. Now I'd like to leave without further lip. The choice is yours."

He came lightly across the deck and hopped up on the pier about three feet from me. "Don't call me shorty, peeper."

I said reasonably, "O.K., we'll sign a pact. You don't call me peeper and I won't call you shorty. Agreed?"

He maintained the idiotic grin of the short man's happy-warrior type. "Do I still look small to you?"

He was wide and his forearms were ridged with muscle. I said wearily, "I never called you small. But admit it: you're about five feet eight inches. That's *short*."

He expanded his chest. "Why don't you try me, fatso?"

Little men. . . . I don't know what bugs them. This Chavez must have weighed about one eighty, and he was undoubtedly fast, tough, and durable. Was that enough? No. He had to be sensitive about his height.

"It wouldn't be fair for me to fight you," I said. "Now slow down and crawl under your rock again."

"Beat it, yellowbelly," he said hoarsely.

Enough, enough. . . . I wasn't quite sure what I had in mind, but I took a step toward him and he pulled back a clenched right hand. And as he did I realized his arms were thick but sadly short.

I reached out with my left hand before he could throw that big right. I found a firm grip on his Adam's apple.

He gagged as he threw the right wildly. He tried to pull his throat clear, but I stayed with him, squeezing hard. His knees began to buckle and he chopped at my forearm with one hand while he tried to pull my wrist away with the other.

I walked him right to the edge of the pier and dumped him.

I had misjudged. He went off backward and he was too close to the boat. His head hit the hull with a horrible *thunk* before he splashed into the harbor.

There was a ninety per cent chance that he had been unconscious when he had hit the water. I bent to take off my shoes. And then, as I cursed a knotted lace, I saw a man come from the ship's cabin.

He was over the railing and into the water before I could untie the snarled knot. I stood up.

Both of them came bobbing to the surface and the new man called, "There's a rope on deck. Get it quick and throw us an end!"

I jumped aboard to get the rope, the face of the new man stirring a memory in my mind. It was a slightly older replica of the face in the picture Bud had given me.

I had finally found Skip Lund.

EIGHT

Skip Lund stepped into a dry pair of dungarees. "Blame me. I was listening. Pete's—uh, I don't know. Something's always bugging him. He's been a good friend to me, though."

He was tall and fairly thin, this Warren Temple Lund the Second. He had a mobile face and an engaging grin and I could guess he might be a difficult man to dislike.

We were in the cabin and Pete Chavez, still soaking wet, was lying on a bunk, his eyes closed, the smell of vomit strong. He had swallowed sea water, going under unconscious.

Skip glanced at him and back at me. "I'm sorry about Bud. I should have prepared him for this trip. I—well, I didn't—"

"When did you get back?" I asked.

"This morning." He went over to mop Pete's face with a towel. His back was to me when he said, "How's—my wife?"

"I guess she's all right. You're getting a divorce, I hear."

"That's right." He turned to face me. "They been brainwashing you up there at the house?"

"Who?"

"June and her rich friends."

I shrugged.

He took a breath. "I'll bet that Glenys painted a picture for you, huh? The hot-rodder, she always called me."

"You were, weren't you?"

He sat down and pulled on a pair of sneakers. "Mr. Callahan, I came out of Oklahoma at the tender age of fourteen without a dime in my pocket. At the age of twenty-three I had a filling station that was pumping seventy thousand gallons a month. I had six full-time employees. I netted eleven thousand two hundred dollars out of that station the year I married June."

"Why are you telling me this?" I asked. "My job is over."

He grinned. "I was always a fan of yours. I thought there was a possibility you could root for me, for a change."

"Go on," I said.

"To some people," he went on, "eleven thousand two hundred dollars isn't much. To a plow jockey from Oklahoma, it looked like the heavy lettuce." He inhaled. "To a Christopher, it's lunch money."

"Did it take you twelve years to find that out?"

"I'm not real bright," he admitted, "and damned stubborn." His jaw ridged. "And I was in love."

"And still are."

He said nothing. From the bunk, Pete Chavez muttered something and Skip rose quickly and went over to him.

"Easy, buddy," he said softly. "Everything's under control. Rest. You're going to be all right."

He came back to sit down again. "All right, we moved up here. We got in with that drinking crowd in Montevista. June changed. Maybe I did. It takes two to fight, doesn't it?"

I looked at the bunk. "Not if one of them is Pete Chavez."

I stood up. "Well, you had better phone the police or go in. They think you went up to that cabin with Johnny."

"I know what they think and why they think it," he said. "To hell with them!"

"You'll call Bud, won't you?"

"Of course." He wrinkled his nose. "Let's get out of this stink. What's your hurry? Let's go up on deck."

"My job is done," I told him. "My only charity case."

"Slow down," he said easily. "You sound like Pete."

We went up the two steps to the deck, into the bright sun and clean salt air. From the direction of the lunch stand out on the pier, I saw the glint of glasses. The counterman was watching us.

Lund sighed. "I suppose old brown-nose Bernie has been filling you full of bull about me, too."

"Vogel, you mean? He told me if I asked any more questions around this town, I'd be in trouble. He and I don't seem to hit it off."

"You're not rich," Lund explained. "Brown-nose Bernie can't afford friends like us." He stared out across the water. "I suppose you'll be going back to Los Angeles now?"

"Tomorrow, probably."

Lund continued to stare out across the water. "I wonder why the law isn't here now? They know I have a boat. The harbor master must have alerted them this morning." He turned to face me. "I can't tell them where I've been."

"Then you're in big trouble," I said.

"I know." He faced me squarely. "Don't jump to conclusions. I think what I'm doing is *right*. I don't expect the law to think so. That's why I need you."

"At a hundred a day and expenses?"

"At whatever you charge. The boss will pay it."

"The boss? You're working?"

"You'll get your money. I want you to find Johnny's

killer. Vogel and his buddies couldn't find a load of manure in a phone booth. And Vogel maybe won't want to. Nor will his chum, the D.A. Callahan, I really need you. I haven't got an alibi."

"I don't think they'll let me work in this town, Skip. They don't trust me."

"You'll be bringing me in. That ought to earn you some points."

"Maybe. And can you tell me what you're doing that the law doesn't think is right?"

He shook his head. "If I could, I wouldn't need you."

What did I expect for a hundred a day, the easy ones? The FBI got those. I said, "A hundred a day, expenses—and a promise from you."

"Name it."

"That if you and June get a divorce and June gets custody, you'll still see Bud every day you're in town."

"I'd do that anyway," he said. "It's a deal."

Chief Chandler Harris was in his office. He sat behind his desk and glared at both of us. Finally he managed to say, "Well!"

"This is my client, Warren Lund," I said quietly. "He has just learned that you have been looking for him."

"Your client? Since when? What's going on here?"

"He came to me," I half lied, "with the understanding that if he gave himself up I would try to find out who killed Johnny Chavez. Of course, I'd need your permission to work on that. In town, anyway. I'm sure the Sheriff's Department would co-operate in the county."

"If he has an alibi," Harris said coldly, "why does he need you?"

"Because Johnny was my friend," Skip answered for me. "I've got an alibi—Johnny's own cousin."

"Pete Chavez?" The chief snorted contemptuously. "Is he all you can come up with?"

"My God!" Lund said. "He and Johnny were more than cousins; they've been buddies for twenty years. You don't think Pete would cover for Johnny's murderer, do you?"

Harris looked between us and settled on Lund. "What day is the alibi for—the day Chavez was killed?"

Tricky. Skip probably didn't know what day Johnny had died.

"For the past two weeks I've been with Pete. Since the day Johnny went up to the cabin."

"Where were you with Pete?"

"On the boat."

"Without any other witnesses, out on the ocean?"

"We have a log," Johnny said.

"Written by you or by Pete? How in hell could that be an alibi? Listen, Lund, you told Mary Chavez you were going up to that cabin with her brother. A log is no alibi. And Pete Chavez is a bad witness."

"I lied to Mary," Lund said stubbornly. "Johnny and I both lied to her about going to the cabin together."

I could see the inevitable question coming before Harris voiced it.

Harris asked simply, "Why did you lie?"

A silence. Skip looked helplessly at me and I said, "You'll need a lawyer. But phone Bud first. He's been waiting a long time." I looked at the chief. "May my client make two phone calls?"

"One," Harris said.

Lund looked at me again. I said, "What's your lawyer's name?"

"Joseph Farini." He spelled the last name for me.

"I'll talk with him," I said. "You phone Bud." I started for the door.

And Chief Harris said, "Where do you think you're going?"

I turned to stare at him. "Out. To work."

"You think you're in the clear?"

I said patiently, "Am I not? And if not, why not?"

His white hair seemed to bristle and his voice was edgy with suppressed emotion. "Every police officer in this town has been looking for Lund. And you casually bring him in. Doesn't that smell?"

"Not to me. Could you make it clearer, sir?"

"Where'd you find him?"

"On his boat. His friend told me he wasn't there, at first, but Mr. Lund decided to show himself and make this deal with me."

"But you went to the boat. Didn't Sergeant Vogel warn you to stop asking our citizens questions?"

"He did, sir. In a moment of unreasonable anger." I walked slowly back to the desk. "If I am being charged with something, sir, I would like to be represented by counsel."

Almost half a minute of a heavy, alien silence, and then he said quietly, "I'm not charging you with anything yet. I'm warning you to stop investigating this murder."

"But, Chief, I promised my client I'd—"

He raised a hand heavily. "You've had the word. Beat it!"

I looked at Lund. "I couldn't forsee this, Skip, or I wouldn't have promised you. I'll fight it. I can work with the county."

"You're dead," he told me. "I know these people. Get Farini on it. You did what you could. I'm not blaming you." He stared dully at the floor.

And Harris asked me, "What was that crack about county? Who do you think you are, Callahan?"

I said evenly, "You already know who I am, sir; you

checked me. The word 'county' was used in a *private* aside to my client about a case outside your jurisdiction. May I go now?"

His pudgy face held nothing but malevolence and his voice was pure threat. "Go. Check with the sheriff. I'm calling him now." He reached for the phone on his desk.

I said to Skip, "You'll hear from me. Call Bud."

Pointless official arrogance, bred of resentments I had had no part in shaping, a small man in a job growing too big. But his local power wasn't diminished by these lacks, and his contempt for people of less power was a nourishment he needed for his insubstantial ego.

I drove out to Montevista.

My client was throwing a ball to his contemporary when I drove in between the chipped stucco pillars. He was at the side of my car by the time I had turned off the ignition.

"Pop called! He said everything is going to be all right. Is it, Brock?"

I said, "If I'm lucky and justice triumphs."

"What does that mean?"

"It means I'm still working."

He studied me doubtfully and then his companion came over. The boy was taller and huskier than Bud and moved with an athlete's grace, but I was sure he didn't have Bud's potential.

Bud said, "This is Don Boyer, Brock. This is Mr. Brock Callahan, Don."

The kid's eyes bugged. "The *Rock?*"

These were the discerning ones. Not Chief Harris or those dopes at Officer Candidate School or San Francisco sports writers. These were the clear minds and unprejudiced judgments.

I said, "It was only a nickname." I held out a hand. "Glad to know any friend of Bud's, Don."

"Jeepers!" he said wonderingly. "Holy cow!"

He was maybe overplaying it a shade, but I needed it after that session with Harris. I said, "Thank you. Would you excuse Bud for a few minutes? We have some private things to discuss."

"Sure," he said. "Natch. Jeepers . . ."

Bud and I walked out of the circle of his adulation, around a corner of the house to the side yard.

There I told him, "Bud, right now your father is being held by the police. You see, the police think your father was with this Chavez when he was killed."

"Was he?"

I shook my head. "He was—doing some work he can't tell the police about."

"What kind of work?"

"I don't know, Bud."

"Maybe it's secret, do you think? I mean, like for the government . . . ?"

"Your father wouldn't tell me," I said. "So now I have to find the man who killed this Chavez so your father won't have to answer all those questions for the police."

He seemed to be holding his breath. He still wore his glove and he kept pounding the ball into it, thinking thoughts he may have been afraid to voice.

"Chin up," I said. "We're going to come out all right."

And then, from a window above us, the well-bred voice of Glenys Christopher called, "Time for lunch, Bud. Who's out there?"

"Mr. Callahan," he said.

"Well, invite him to lunch," she said. "And Don can stay, too."

He went to get his friend; I went around to the front door. Glenys was waiting for me there. Her smile was warm, if self-conscious.

"You didn't need my help, luckily. You found Skip."

"I found him. What did you mean by 'luckily'? Couldn't you reach Ritter?"

"I reached him halfway through his game of golf and he wasn't very reasonable." She sighed. "I probably caught him at a bad time."

"Did he refuse to speak with Harris about me?"

"Not quite that bluntly. He said he didn't think his one term as mayor gave him the right to interfere in the operation of the Police Department."

"Double talk," I said. "Who asked him to *interfere?*"

She rested a hand on my arm. "It doesn't matter now, anyway, does it? You've found Skip."

"And he hired me to find Chavez' killer. Can I do that without Department co-operation?"

She stared at me quietly. "He hired you? You don't think—" She broke off, frowning.

"Think he killed Chavez?" I finished for her. "I don't."

"Bernie does."

"That's why your brother-in-law hired me. Is there any Einlicher around?"

"I guess." She studied me anxiously. "What's wrong? You seem about ready to blow up."

"It's been a stinking morning. Let's have a beer and I'll tell you about it."

June was downtown at some luncheon and the kids wanted to watch TV while they ate. So Glenys and I had lunch alone in the sunroom next to the side patio.

I told her how I had found Skip Lund, deleting the violence. And I went on to relate my words with Chief Chandler Harris and then remembered that I had promised to phone Skip's lawyer.

I did that and came back to the table to find Glenys

looking bleakly out at the patio.

"I shouldn't have come in," I said. "Now my mood has soured you."

She shook her head. "No. I was thinking of June. I think she's still in love with Skip."

"And that makes you blue?"

"Shouldn't it? What is he? Look at his friends."

I said, "Some fine men have unusual friends. As to what Skip is—he was a self-made man earning a cool eleven grand a year when he married your sister. Who made him what he is now?"

Her face stiffened and she stared at me angrily.

"A poor kid," I went on grimly, "who is earning eleven thousand a year at the age of twenty-three is *not a bum*. I like this Lund. He went wrong somewhere, maybe, but I like him one hell of a lot better than James Edward Ritter."

"You would. He's your type—a roughneck."

"Maybe. Whatever that means. He's not the kind who can live on his wife's money without being corrupted."

"Who forced him to live on June's money?"

"I don't know," I said. "You tell me."

"It was Skip's idea, moving up here," she said.

"Up here means San Valdesto. Was Montevista his choice, too?"

She exhaled heavily. "I—don't know. I suppose not."

From the TV in the den came the sounds of gunfire and horses' hooves and the shouts of western heroes. "Throw down your gun and come out, Baxter! You're surrounded."

Aren't we all, I thought; *aren't we all. . . .*

Tears moved slowly down the brown cheeks of Glenys Christopher and her long-fingered hands were clenched on top of the table.

I said softly, "I didn't accuse you of changing Skip Lund, Glenys. That isn't what I was trying to say, not this time.

I meant, well—hell—*money*—"

"I know!" She stood up and left the table.

Money. It had brought Roger Scott into her life and probably the fink she had married. It had attracted the nothing men to her and now was breaking up a marriage in her family.

She came back with a piece of Kleenex, and I said, "Bobby turned out all right, thanks to you. June will have to run her own life."

She dabbed at her eyes and her nose. She didn't look at me. She sat down and sipped her coffee.

From the den came the shouted merits of a crispy, crunchy, tasty, nutty, high-vitamin, low-calorie, and completely worthless breakfast food. Across from me, Glenys sniffed.

"That Bud's a good kid," I said. "Gutty and honest. Handsome, too. And you're a very attractive woman. Things aren't *all* bad."

"Shut up!" she said. "I wasn't thinking of any of those things." Her voice was low, intense. "Damn you. Damn you all to hell!"

I stared, mouth agape.

"I promised Jan I'd keep an eye on you, damn you!" she stormed. "Oh, you sly son-of-a-bitch!"

It was the wrong time, but I had to laugh.

And finally she had to join me.

Because, for sure, she had kept an eye on me, on much more of me than she had ever promised Jan.

NINE

I HAD BEEN warned against doing any further investigating, but what could Harris prove? If I asked some stalwart citizen questions, Harris might have a case. But the kind of people who were involved in the local life of Skip Lund weren't people who would be likely to complain to the Department. And I wanted to talk with Mary Chavez.

Her place, not more than two or three blocks from Chickie's, was a brown-and-yellow frame cottage, flanking a lumberyard, smothered in bougainvillaea and geraniums. I had to park a block away; both sides of the street were banked with mourners' cars.

I sat there, realizing that it would be in bad taste to wade through all those mourners at the house just to ask the deceased man's sister some questions. She had come to me after he had died, but going through those mourners made it seem different.

I was about to leave again when a Ford pickup parked behind me and Pete Chavez, somber in a serge suit, stepped out of it and started down the walk toward the house.

I opened my door on the curb side and called to him.

He stayed on the sidewalk, glaring at me.

I said, "Skip hired me. Didn't he tell you?"

"So? That don't make us buddies, Callahan. Skip's crazy, lining up with you."

"I'd like to speak with Mary," I said. "Would you tell her?"

He sneered and shook his head.

"I have a message for her," I lied, "from Skip. A *private* message."

"You're lying," he said.

"Believe what you want," I said quietly. "I'll wait here five minutes. If she comes, O.K. If she doesn't, you can explain to Skip why you wouldn't help. So long."

He smiled cynically, muttered something, and continued toward the house.

Three minutes later Mary Chavez was hurrying down my way. She was completely in black, including hat and veil. Her enormous eyes were free of tears.

She asked in that cello voice, "Is Skip going to be all right?"

"We can hope. Mary, if I'm going to do him any good, I'll need all the help I can get. Why do you think Skip lied to you about going to that cabin?"

She studied me fearfully. "Won't he tell you?"

"He wouldn't. Who is he working for? He said something about a boss. Have you any idea who that could be?"

She stared at me and then past me as a squad car went slowly by. "What are they doing here?"

"Just cruising, I suppose. I didn't bring them."

She watched the car until it was out of sight and then looked back at me. "I don't know what my brother and Skip were doing. Why doesn't Skip want to tell you?"

I shrugged. "You can't help? Do you think it might be narcotics, Mary?"

She stared at me doubtfully. "Who told you that? Where did you hear that?"

"Nobody told me. It's a pattern that's been forming in my mind. Do you have any reason to think it might be a sound guess?"

She shook her head slowly. "Though it would be a good business in this end of town. But not Skip, no . . ."

"Haven't you wondered?" I persisted. "I should think if you and Skip were serious about getting married, you would have talked about his business."

"Talk to Pete," she said. "Talk to Skip. They don't tell me *anything!*"

"O.K. I guess Skip is wasting his money, hiring me. I can't help him—not without some help. Well, goodbye."

She didn't move. She stood there in the hot sun, small, black-garbed, beautiful, and desolate.

I turned on the ignition and started the engine. And she said, "Talk to Juanita. If she wants to help you, she can. She has to help you."

"Why, if you won't? Goodbye, Mary."

I stalled, but no further words came from her. She still hadn't started back for the house when I pulled away; she seemed lost in thought.

Her brother dead for reasons unknown to her and Skip apparently taking the same road that her brother had followed. She had enough to think about.

She was an innocent, I felt sure. And because she was, Skip had been forced to lie about going to the cabin with her brother. It could mean only that he needed an acceptable excuse for a trip that he couldn't reveal to her. And wouldn't reveal to me.

I stopped at a drugstore and bought a carton of cigarettes. Harris had told me not to investigate the murder, so he would have reason to prevent me from talking with Skip.

But certainly I had a right to bring a friend a carton of cigarettes.

Harris wasn't at Headquarters. The sergeant at the desk looked at me doubtfully and said, "Lund's attorney is with him now. Maybe you'd better wait until he comes out."

"I only need a few minutes," I said. "And I'd like to meet his attorney."

The man hesitated and then said quietly, "O.K. Five minutes."

Attorney Joseph Farini was an enormous man, as tall as I was and at least fifty pounds heavier. In Skip's cell he shook my hand and shared my sentiment; we weren't going to do Skip any good with the information he was willing to give us.

"I was with Johnny's cousin," Skip protested. "How much alibi does a man need? You're telling me, as a *lawyer*, that you can't successfully defend an innocent man?"

Farini said heavily, "I can defend you, innocent or guilty. I like to have as many weapons as I can in *any* defense. And an *evasive* innocent man makes a poor client. The police and the prosecution are going to hammer at your alibi—the trip. And your refusing to tell *why* you took the trip is a highly vulnerable point."

"Especially," I added, "when you had already told Miss Chavez that you were going to the cabin with Johnny."

Farini nodded agreement.

Skip said, "Mary won't repeat that story under oath."

Farini asked, "Will she *lie* under oath?"

"No. She'll refuse to answer that question."

"On what grounds?"

Skip shrugged. "That's your job—to give her grounds."

I said, "You admitted to Harris that you told Mary that. Harris is a pretty substantial witness for the state, Skip." I looked at Farini. "Maybe I'd have better luck if Skip and I were alone."

He shrugged. "Maybe. I'll wait for you, Mr. Callahan."

The turnkey let him out and told me gruffly, "Three more minutes, Callahan. Sergeant's orders."

Farini frowned. "What's this? Which sergeant?"

"The sergeant at the desk," I told him. "Perhaps a word from you, Mr. Farini . . . ?"

"He'll hear 'em," the big man promised. "Take all the goddamned time you like." And, to the turnkey, "You come with me, officer."

Skip was smiling as they went down the corridor.

"Must be a big man," I said. "Where'd you get him?"

"We go fishing together. I have a *few* rich friends, Callahan."

"All right," I said, "he's gone. And only this crummy private eye can hear you. What's your racket?"

He stared at the cell floor. "It was never that, not to me. I'm sorry I ever got into it, but I never thought of it as a racket, believe me." He lifted his eyes to face me earnestly. "I can't tell you. That much I still owe the people involved."

"I can guess it isn't political," I said, "and involves a boat. That could mean running booze or pearls or wetbacks."

No sign of interest in his face.

"Or dope," I threw at him.

A flicker in his eyes.

"Dope?" I repeated.

"You're wasting your time."

"O.K." I said patiently, "we won't name it. Let's just assume for the moment that it's illegal. Now, if Chavez was in it, too, it could be the reason he died. Does that make sense?"

"It doesn't make sense to me, but it's a possibility."

"So Johnny went to the cabin alone. Why did he go there? It's not deer country and it wasn't deer season."

"I don't know why Johnny went there, so help me."

"Maybe he went there to meet somebody," I suggested.

He nodded. "That could easily be. He was a real quiff hound, that Johnny. Some dame, you mean?"

"No. I wasn't thinking of a woman. I've been told that Johnny had some contact with the L.A. emigrants up here—some hoodlum contacts. Maybe Johnny was arranging a meeting with the competition—and was double-crossed." I looked at him questioningly.

"Oh, no," he said. "You're reaching now."

"I have to. I'm working blind, thanks to you. Do you have any better theories?"

He shook his head slowly, staring past me. "I've been trying to come up with something ever since I heard about it. I heard it on the radio while we were still at sea. Hell, for a whole day Pete and I didn't talk about anything else. And Pete's as much in the dark as I am. But he's going to look into it, you can be damned sure."

"The reason I keep thinking about dope," I said, "is because Johnny Chavez served time for selling reefers to high-school kids."

He stared at me in shock. "That's a lie. When?"

"A few years back, probably before you knew him."

"Are you sure, Callahan?"

"Yes."

"God!" He sat on the bunk and stared at the carton of cigarettes I'd brought him. He looked up. "Cripes, I never knew that. Hell, Johnny wasn't like that *at all!*"

"He was a friend. You weren't critical. Knowing that, can you now believe Johnny might have been planning a double cross up in that cabin?"

"If that's true—what you told me—I don't know what

the hell to believe. Has Pete—what kind of record has Pete got?"

"I don't know. When the police here were co-operative, I hadn't heard of Pete Chavez. Since this morning, I'm not likely to get a chance to look at the files."

He still seemed shocked by my revelation about Johnny Chavez. I had a feeling he also felt conned.

I said, "A revolt against Montevista mores didn't have to go as far as a *racket*, did it?"

He didn't answer.

I asked, "Is there a possibility that Pete Chavez would work with me? He's not a logical member of my fan club."

"I don't know," he said wearily. "You can tell him I hired you."

"I already have. It didn't help. Well, I'll try again. You still aren't ready to open up and help your own cause?"

His voice was dull. "If I opened up, I'd get ten years. I think I've been a sucker, Callahan, though I'm not completely sure—not yet. I wish I could help you. If you want to quit, I'll understand."

"I never quit," I told him. "Though I often lose. Chin up; you're still breathing."

I didn't think it was politic to add that I had former clients who weren't.

In the front room, Farini was waiting on a bench. He said, "Any luck?"

"None. Can you throw your weight around here some more and learn if Pete Chavez has any record?"

"I've already checked him," he told me. "Traffic violations; that's all."

"The way Chief Harris talked, I had the impression that Pete would make an unacceptable witness for the defense. Does he have a bad rep?"

"He's Johnny's cousin; that's enough." Farini rubbed the

back of his thick neck. "You have no lead, have you? No place to start?"

"Maybe. I'd rather not reveal it to a man hindered by ethics. In my world, I've evolved my own code. The Bar Association has established yours. Did you have any people in mind I might contact?"

"None," he said. "Corporation law is my field. But I like this Skip Lund and I think he's worth straightening out. He got a bad start up here."

"He tells me he was a solid citizen in Beverly Hills," I said.

"He was," Farini said. "I checked that, too." He smiled. "Skip was a friend, but a lawyer is a lawyer. You know, when I was younger your trade appealed to me."

I returned his smile. "Joe, you're big enough for it, but I don't think you're dumb enough. Well, back to the jute mill." I shook his hand. "If the police get obnoxious, I'll know who to call."

I went out into the day again, and two cars down from mine a red Porsche was parked. June Lund was coming along the sidewalk toward me. I waited.

The blue eyes under the chestnut hair were clear and young this afternoon. Her chin lifted when she recognized me.

"Hello," I said. "It must have been a long luncheon."

She frowned.

"Glenys told me about it," I explained, "but it's four o'clock now."

"I had some shopping to do," she said. "Are you checking up on my actions, Mr. Callahan?"

"No, ma'am," I said. "Only making polite conversation."

She asked gravely, "How is Skip? Is he all right? Is—I mean, will they be holding him long?"

"He's healthy," I said. "I think at the moment, he's regretting the path he took after leaving the Montevista boozers.

Could you live on eleven thousand two hundred dollars a
year, Mrs. Lund?"

Her chin stayed high. "I suppose. But I don't have to.
Will it be enough for Mary Chavez? It should be a step *up*
for her."

I said nothing.

She said, "All right; I didn't have to say that. Not to you,
anyway. But he is going to marry her, isn't he?"

I shrugged.

"I heard that he was taking instructions," she said, "that
he was going to turn Catholic. I heard it was all settled.
Didn't you learn that?"

"I heard it. I don't believe everything I hear. What's your
church, Mrs. Lund?"

"Don't lecture me," she said. "You're not qualified.
What's *your* church, Mr. Callahan?"

I smiled. "Let's not fight. You're here; that's the first
step. We can always fight later."

"I'm here," she informed me coolly, "to tell that retarded
hot-rodder exactly what I think of a man who neglects to
maintain contact with his own son. I'm here to give that
arrogant idiot a piece of my mind."

"Sure you are," I said. "Hell, yes. Good luck, Mrs. Lund."

It was only a little after four o'clock, but I was hungry.
Juanita had bragged about her enchiladas. Perhaps I could
kill two birds with one beer. Coming at her with direct
questions had availed me little, but maybe I'd be luckier if
I gave her more time.

On a Saturday afternoon one would expect a working-
man's bar like Chickie's to be well populated. It wasn't,
when I entered. There was a short, thick, and dark man
with a scar under his right eye working the bar.

At a table near the entrance to the kitchen the lanky guitar
player was playing cards with two shorter, heavier men.

The bartender asked quietly, "What'll it be, sir?"

"A beer for now. Enchiladas a little later. Is Mrs. Rico here?"

"She's in the kitchen. Did you wish to speak to her?"

"It can wait. Draught beer."

He poured a glass and set it in front of me and went over to stand near the cash register. It was quiet in here, the distant, hushed crackle of frying food in the kitchen, the halfhearted buzzing of a fly, the scarcely audible slap of playing cards. But under the lazy passing of time I felt a tension.

"Quiet town, isn't it?" I said to the bartender.

"Mostly. Quieter than down south. I like it."

"Lot of money in this town," I added.

He smiled sadly. "Not in this end of it. Plan to open a business here?"

At the table one of the men said something in Spanish and the other two laughed. They probably weren't talking about me, but I felt uncomfortable. The bartender glanced at me doubtfully, and away. That was the tension I probably sensed—the *insularity* here.

I said, "I've got a business already, in Beverly Hills, and I don't plan to move it."

Again there was a remark in Spanish from the table and another laugh. I turned to look that way and one of the heavy men met my gaze steadily, smiling without warmth.

And then the swinging door to the kitchen opened and Juanita stood there, staring at the three men. They gave immediate and complete attention to their cards.

Her smile was warm when she finally looked at me. "Mr. Callahan! Still on vacation?"

"Nope. Working. I thought I'd have some of those enchiladas you were bragging about last night."

"In five minutes," she promised. "Nurse your beer. In

five minutes you'll see if I was bragging." The door swung shut.

The men at the table continued their game quietly. The bartender commented, "Best enchiladas in town."

"Good. Another beer."

A man and woman came in. Filipinos. The man wore a sport jacket composed of all the colors there are; the woman was small and shapely in tight black silk. They took a table as far as possible from the card players.

The woman in black made me think of Mary Chavez, and I wondered if she was still bearing up or if grief had finally pierced her composure. Perhaps she and her wild brother had grown apart. While she had gone to school to learn typing, he had set out on the trail of the fast buck.

And wound up being nibbled by rats.

Sadness and an uneasy peace, the beer putting a blurred benediction on the day. The man and his woman talked softly; the smell of food from the kitchen stirred my hunger.

And then the front door opened once more and Lars (Red) Hovde stood there, grinning apishly at us all. The slob hadn't even changed his crummy sport shirt.

"Back again," he said happily. "Start the music, professor!"

~~~~~~~~~~~~~~~ *TEN* ~~~~~~~~~~~~~~~

HE CAME OVER to where I sat and I managed to nod civilly.

"Callahan," he said genially. "Didn't expect to see you here."

"Why not, Red?" I asked. "I wasn't knifed or slugged."

"They weren't from here," he said scornfully. "These are my friends." He called to the men playing cards, "Right?"

Without looking up, the guitar player said, *"Si, amigo."*

"Gracias, gracias," Red said, and looked smugly at me. "I even got the lingo now." He climbed up on the stool next to mine. He slapped the bar. "Double bourbon, buddy."

He was about half-gassed already. I could smell the sweet wine on his breath. Sweet wine and bourbon—what a mess he was going to be. I didn't want to move away from him too obviously; I sat where I was.

He relished the alliteration of his order and repeated it. "Double bourbon, buddy. If I can say that, I'm not drunk, huh?"

"Right. I thought you were in the hospital. I heard you were knifed."

"Hell," he said, "I've cut myself worse than that shaving. Where's Juanita?"

"In the kitchen, making enchiladas. You gave Vogel my name, didn't you?"

"Vogel? Oh, that cop? Yeah. I was drunk. He give you a bad time?"

I shook my head.

Red called loudly, "Hey, Juanita!"

Everyone in the room stared, and then Juanita was standing in the open kitchen doorway. "Oh, God!" she said bleakly. "Tanglefoot is back. Good evening, Mr. Hovde."

"When does the dancing start?" he wanted to know.

"Later," she told him. "Much later. It's not even five o'clock, Mr. Hovde." She closed the door again.

The bartender set the double jolt in front of him and Lars said to me, "She don't fool me. I was getting to her last night. *Mr. Hovde*, huh! You should have hung around. You have a date or something?"

I shook my head. "I didn't want to miss Jack Paar."

"Jack Paar," Red said scornfully. "He don't fool me." He lifted the double shot and gulped it down.

It had been too unpleasant a day for me to sit next to this freak and listen to him detail the list of people who didn't fool *him*. But if I moved away, his aggressive sense of inferiority might be triggered into pugnacious action, and it was no time for a fight. I was cornered.

"Double bourbon, buddy," he said again, holding his glass high.

And then I saw a chance to get away. Because Juanita was coming from the kitchen, a steaming plate in her hands, and I assumed that it held my enchiladas.

I slipped from the stool and beckoned to her as I headed for the smallest table in the room, a corner table.

She nodded understandingly as she followed my lead.

She put the plate on the table and said, "Isn't he awful? I'll get my plate and some lettuce." She went back to the kitchen.

She returned in a few minutes with a big bowl of ice-cold chopped lettuce and a plate for herself. The table was crowded with the two of us; there wasn't an inch of room for Hovde.

He hadn't missed me yet; he was trying out his new three-word Spanish vocabulary on the bartender.

Juanita said, "Skip turned himself in, I hear."

I nodded and dug into an enchilada. "Wonderful!" I said. "You weren't bragging."

"Thank you. Are they trying to railroad Skip downtown?"

I shrugged. "He isn't helping himself much. He claims he was on some kind of trip, but that's all he's willing to say about it."

"Oh?" Her voice was casual, but she had stopped eating.

I looked at her directly and asked, "Would you know what kind of trip it was?"

Her voice was tight. "Why should I?"

"That's no answer. Skip has hired me to find Johnny's killer. I'm not going to get any help from the police on it. Am I going to get any from you?"

"You're talking nonsense, *amigo*," she said in her deep voice. "Skip and Johnny were close friends. A hundred people will tell the judge that, or the police. Skip could *never* be convicted."

"You'd like to believe. Let me tell you, Juanita, if I don't come up with the murderer, the police are going to put a lot of pressure on Warren Temple Lund the Second."

Silence. She was less angry than thoughtful, it seemed, but there was some anger in her dark eyes. I ate some of the cold lettuce and some more enchilada. I glanced toward the bar to see Lars Hovde studying us speculatively.

"Don't look now," I whispered to Juanita, "but Red is watching us. If he gets belligerent, I'm going to pop him."

"No," she said firmly. "I already had enough trouble with the police about him. I can't afford any trouble now."

"No trouble," I assured her. "One punch and he'll be asleep."

"No. No, no, no! Please?"

Red was getting carefully off his stool now and walking over.

"Please," Juanita said urgently. "I'll handle this."

"O.K."

She looked up with a big smile as he walked over with the deliberate pace of the conscious drunk.

He missed the smile; his attention was on me. "Callahan, you're asking for trouble. You don't fool me."

"I wouldn't try to fool you, Red," I said. "Calm down."

Juanita said quickly and warmly. "Red, the night is young. Mr. Callahan and I have very important business to discuss, but it won't take long."

He looked at her suspiciously.

She said softly, "No trouble now, Lars. We don't want the police in here, do we?"

"Hell, no," he agreed. He studied me carefully for a few seconds and then smiled at her. "But if this guy gets fresh, you holler. O.K.?"

She nodded.

He winked at her, sneered at me, and went over to where the men were playing cards. I fought the annoyance in me.

"Deal me in," he said to the players. And, to the bartender, "Drinks for this table on me. *Mucho.*" He sat down heavily.

Juanita said, "For two months he says nothing but 'double bourbon.' I wish he'd never learned to talk."

"I wonder who worked him over last night."

She smiled. "Always digging, digging, digging, aren't you?"

"That's why my clients pay me," I told her. "Right now, all I'm trying to do is save Skip Lund's neck. People who hire private investigators usually have some reason why they can't go directly to the police, but Skip's secrecy could destroy his alibi."

"He'll be all right," she said. "He always lands on his feet."

I said irritably, "Don't be so damned smug. Johnny Chavez was murdered. Keep that in mind. Wasn't he a friend of yours?"

She nodded, her eyes sad and angry. "He's dead. The world goes on. I cry for the living, not the dead."

"I don't think you cry for *anybody*."

She stared at me, her eyes now hard. She stood up. "I'll get our coffee. You watch your tongue, Brock Callahan."

I watched her walk toward the kitchen, enough woman for anyone. I was sorry my frustration had made me tactless.

She came back with two mugs and an enameled coffeepot. "Cream or sugar?"

"Neither," I said. "I apologize, Juanita. It's been a sour day."

"Of course," she said calmly. "And why did you come here tonight?"

Because Mary Chavez told me to, I thought. I said, "Because I think you can help Skip Lund and he's my client. And also because if I clear Skip, I help his son. That's the biggest motivation in this mess."

"If you don't work with the police," she said, "you lose your license and you are out of business. You cannot hide things from the police and stay in business."

"Yes, I can. I have before. Justice is not always complete

and perfect, and no reasonable police officer expects it will be."

"In San Valdesto," she said, "the police are not reasonable." She sipped her coffee.

The front door opened and a man came in, the same man I had seen in uniform down at Headquarters, the Mexican patrolman. He wasn't in uniform now.

He waved at Juanita and went to the bar.

She looked from him to me and away.

"Is that your pipeline into Headquarters?" I asked. "Is that how you found out where I was staying?"

She sipped her coffee, ignoring me.

"You called me originally," I reminded her, "and told me you were worried about Skip's son. And you knew where Skip was. That should mean you knew what he was doing. Maybe *what* Skip was doing is involved in *why* Johnny died and maybe not. But I can't work blind!"

Her face was blank, her breathing heavy. She took a cigarette from a pack and I held a light for her.

She inhaled and said, "You don't smoke, do you?"

"Don't change the subject."

"I'm not changing it; I'm ignoring it. I thought you came to eat, not to snoop."

"O.K. To hell with it. If you don't want to help Skip Lund, I'll work without your help." I paused. "And hope you're not involved."

She smoked and sipped her coffee.

"Duddle burden, bubby," Red called to the bartender.

Juanita said angrily, "Damn him! I wish he would leave."

"Durdle bubben, duddy," Red called.

"What is he trying to say?" Juanita asked. "He sounds like he's drowning."

"He is drowning," I said. "In booze. He's trying to order a double bourbon."

Juanita signaled the bartender and caught his eye. She made a gesture with an inverted thumb.

"A Mickey?" I asked quietly. "Dangerous business, Juanita."

"It's Saturday night," she said. "We'll be crowded in another hour. Do I want him around here then, calling people spics? I'm protecting him from himself. I have a cot in the back where he can sleep it off."

I sipped my coffee, ignoring her.

"You're angry," she said.

"Why not? With the help of his friends, I might be able to do Skip Lund and his son some good. And now I learn he has no friends. So I have to go back to him and say I can't honestly take his case because I can't do him any good."

She shook her head and sighed. She studied me a second and then glanced toward the table where Red was now drinking his drugged double bourbon. She gestured to the guitar player and stood up.

At the bar the man out of uniform had his back to us, oblivious to the shenanigans going on behind him, quietly drinking a beer.

Juanita moved a few steps away from the table and talked softly to the guitar player. He nodded and went back to the others. She sat down again and I stood up.

She frowned. "You're not going . . . ?"

"Why not?" I took some bills from my pocket. "How much?"

"Nothing, nothing." She took a breath. "Angry, aren't you?"

"Frustrated. I have to go back and tell Skip I can't do him any good."

At the other table Red had collapsed, his head among the cards. The guitar player and one of his friends lifted him and half carried, half dragged him through the swinging door that led to the kitchen.

The Filipino and his companion laughed nervously, the bartender boredly polished glasses, the man out of uniform continued to drink his beer.

From the kitchen came the sound of excited Spanish words and then an abrupt silence.

I said, "I hope he doesn't get knifed again tonight. A man can only take so much of that."

Juanita's eyes flashed. "You have a nasty tongue."

"I'm an anglo," I explained, "and I am resentful, knowing what you think about angloes. And tonight you're kissing off Skip Lund and Bud Lund and Callahan. Thank you for the free meal and the beer and good night to you, Señora Juanita Rico."

"Damn you!" she said hoarsely. "It's not like that at all. You know those are lies. You have a viper's tongue and a mind like a cop."

"Watch your language," I said. "There's a cop at the bar." I turned my back on her and started out.

I was about three steps from the door when she said, "Please wait. Please?"

I turned and waited.

She came over to put a hand on my arm. "We had a bad start. I guess I can trust you. I won't promise; but will you give me a little time to think about it?"

"All right."

She smiled warmly. "Have a beer and be patient."

Perhaps patience would only give her time to dream up more evasions, but I had no other leads. I couldn't honestly expect her to involve her safety in the affairs of Skip Lund when Lund refused to save his own neck. I went back to the table and another glass of beer.

A couple came in and went to a table. A woman came in

and took the stool next to the police officer in civvies. The guitar player moved his chair into a corner and began to play softly.

Peaceful again, deceptively peaceful. *Mañana* land, and *mañana* was Sunday. It would get festive as the alcohol seeped into the warm blood stream; it might even get violent. But this was the lull before the loving—natural party people slowly warming up.

Beneath the surface sweetness of the quiet guitar there was a beat I couldn't chart, repetitive and constant, unrhythmical, disturbing, trying to say something less soporific than the melody.

Imminence seemed to lurk hazily in the room. Imminence of what? Romance? Revelation? Violence?

I had a sense of being a surface swimmer, only a few feet above the kelp in a calm sea, while beneath the kelp the sharks watched, patient and alert.

Behind the bar Juanita was now helping the bartender. A squat, dark-brown waitress was working out of the kitchen. The Filipino was holding the hand of his beloved in the black dress, blithely oblivious to the urgent undertone of the guitar and the mythical sharks under the kelp.

Over all their heads I watched Juanita working the bar and the tables easily and gracefully, a woman who probably missed nothing, a complete and courageous but still *womanly* woman.

When Skip used the word ''boss'' I was sure that he was speaking of Juanita. That would mean that Johnny had been working for her, too. And Pete Chavez. And what was their trade?

Juanita went to the kitchen and came out in less than a minute, carrying nothing. Had she checked on Hovde? She went to the bar and picked up a pair of drinks to take to the Filipino couple.

And then she was standing in front of me and I rose. The sound of the guitar dwindled off to nothing. I glanced at the player and he returned my stare vacantly, then started another piece.

"What I have decided to tell you must be kept a secret," Juanita warned. "Can you promise me that and still stay in business?"

"Unless it means I have to hide a murderer, I promise you that, whether it's wise or not."

"It might help to find a murderer."

"Then I will keep your secret."

"Have you guessed anything?" she asked musingly.

"I've been thinking of narcotics. It was only a hunch."

"It was a good one," she said, and sat down across from me.

∞∞∞∞∞∞∞∞∞ *ELEVEN* ∞∞∞∞∞∞∞∞∞

SHE GAVE IT to me straight and simple, but it was still a strange story. The boat brought in opium; she had a man who derived the heroin and morphine, a trained man, an addict.

In this end of town, she explained, drug addiction was growing. And why?

"The money in it," I guessed. "Once a man is hooked, he'd do *anything* to get the money for more. So the pushers build the business and get rich."

"And the addicts steal and kill, if they have to, to get the money. And the women turn into prostitutes. It was growing in this end of town."

"*Was* growing? Isn't it any more?"

"There hasn't been a new addict in this neighborhood in three months."

"Why not?"

"Nobody's getting rich from it," she said. "When angloes can't get rich, they get out of a business. They don't want to build new customers for a nonprofit business."

"Don't tell me you gave it away?"

"When we had to. Those who could pay did pay. Those who couldn't pay didn't have to pay. They could owe or take charity. Since we started, we have three addicts who seem to be cured, though one can never be sure. The ones still on it will die, eventually, and there will be no new customers to take their places. Then we can happily go out of business."

"And who moves in?"

She stared at me, frowning.

"Juanita," I said quietly, "wherever there's a big and dirty buck, the slime moves in. And there are ways to get rid of small operators like you. The boys from down south don't like independent wholesalers. It's just a question of time until they move in here."

"They have tried," she said simply. "They have failed."

"It couldn't have been the big boys, then. They never fail." I smiled grimly. "Nonprofit narcotics. Ye gods, Juanita, it sounds un-American!"

"It works in England," she said. "It is working in San Valdesto."

I shook my head. "The Mafia is old and wise and universal. They will never permit it. The idea might spread to the big towns."

"It has worked," she said stubbornly.

"So far." And then I remembered what Harris had said about Chavez' being friendly with the newcomers. And I asked, "Was Johnny Chavez your muscle?"

"What is a *muscle*? Johnny was a friend."

"He's also been a friend to some of the new people up here, the way I heard it."

She frowned. "What new people? Gangsters, hoodlums?"

"That's right. Let's call 'em the doubtful people. Did you trust Johnny?"

"Completely," she said.

"I was thinking that if Johnny ratted to the law, you'd be out of business. And Johnny would then be big with the police *and* the new people. A spender like Johnny wouldn't stay interested in a nonprofit business, would he?"

"You didn't know him," she said. "He got a rotten deal in this town. Johnny was a good boy."

"A *good* boy who sold reefers to high-school kids? Isn't your sentiment clouding your judgment?"

"You didn't know him," she repeated. "He was a willful boy, but a good one, once he saw who his friends were."

"All right. I can't argue against sentiment. But tell me, Juanita, what would you have done if you had learned that he had been double-crossing you?"

She shook her head. "You're talking nonsense again."

I smiled. "Can you handle a .30-.30?"

"I can handle anything that uses bullets," she told me levelly. "I have four rifles. And three shotguns. Make a case out of that, nosy Brock Callahan."

"And never again taste your enchiladas?" I teased her.

"Don't joke."

The low-rent-district Glenys Christopher, taking care of her own. No victim, this girl—and it was a pleasure to sit there and look at her. I was getting a bellyful of victims.

"What are you thinking, sly one?" she asked me.

"About your source," I lied. "Is it constant, down there in Mexico?"

"My father," she explained. "He will live a long time yet. And when he is gone, my brother will be there."

Silence once more. The guitar's beat was a throbbing of blood in hot veins, tight, demanding release. Juanita turned to look at the musician and she spoke in Spanish. The beat went away; the soft, sad melodies came back.

She smiled at me. "It is too early for that kind of music. There is a time for everything, no?"

"Yes," I said. A time to live and a time to die, I thought. Too many beers?

"You're thinking again," she accused me. "You're a moody Irishman, aren't you?"

"A man is dead," I said. "A nothing man, from all I've heard; but he's dead and his death causes complications among the living. You don't think Johnny went to the cabin to meet one of the strangers from down south?"

"No," she said firmly. "And he was not a nothing man. Because he was Mexican, is that why you think of him as nothing?"

"That's not why. I don't have your bigotry, Juanita. I think of him as a basketball player who sold reefers to kids. In my book, that makes him a shtunk—and I don't care what his nationality was. I have a hunch he lusted to be a hot-shot again and tried to sell you out."

She shook her head vehemently, but I thought I saw the beginning of doubt in her eyes.

"Didn't he go with Skip, usually, to Mexico?"

"No. He couldn't stand the ocean. He got seasick."

"And Pete? Do you trust him, too?"

She nodded. "Pete is like you—all temper. But he is a friend."

I had learned what I had almost guessed and gained nothing. Perhaps Pete Chavez knew things that Juanita didn't. Though my chances of getting any information out of that knot-head were remote.

I stood up and said, "Thanks, Juanita, for trusting me. I don't know if it has helped, but it might be a wedge with Pete or Skip."

She looked up at me anxiously. "Go with God, *amigo*. And keep our secret."

"I will." I paused. "That Red Hovde—take it easy with him. He's a jerk but really gone on you, honey."

She sighed. "All the wrong men love Juanita. It is one hell of a world, hey, Irish?"

"At times. Where does Pete Chavez live?"

"In Goleta. But not tonight, I heard. Tonight he is staying in Skip's apartment, here in town. Do you know where that is?"

I had it in my notebook, given to me by Chief Harris while he had still been semico-operative. I nodded.

"There is probably a girl there," she explained. "He may not answer."

I nodded again.

"And watch your tongue," she said gravely. "He is very tough, that one."

"So I've been told. I'll be polite. Good night and thank you."

As I went out, the beat of the guitar changed once more. *Goodbye,* it seemed to be saying. *Get lost.*

His beloved cousin lying cold among the mourners and Pete Chavez in the hay with a broad. A realist. His buddy in the clink, so why waste the apartment?

Well, why not? No tears bring back the dead. Get as hot as you can; you're a long time cold. The opiate of the orgasm.

It was a warm night. Shadows hid the grimness of the neighborhood, showing only the warm light through the window, from where came the happy sounds of the poor man's cocktail hour. A slight, dry breeze whispered in the eucalyptus overhead. The stars were bright.

It was not quite seven o'clock; perhaps Pete hadn't reached his borrowed love nest yet. I drove over to the apartment almost hoping he wouldn't be there.

It was true adobe ranch, an old place, four units in a row next to a new medical building. The front doors all faced on a covered, ground-level porch that served as a walk.

There was no bell. I knocked.

I heard footsteps over a stone floor and then the door opened and a stocky, well-used imitation blonde stared out at me.

"I'm looking for Pete Chavez," I explained. "Is he here?"

"Not yet," she said. "He phoned a couple minutes ago and said he was picking up a bottle on the way. You a friend of his?"

"I'm a friend of Skip Lund's," I said.

"Come in, come in," she said genially. "Any friend of Skip's is a friend of mine."

I came into a high-ceilinged, rough-stone-floored utility apartment, complete with day bed, still unopened.

"You like Skip, eh?" I asked.

"I get goose bumps thinking of that hunk of wonderful flesh. But he's so hot for Mary Chavez, he wouldn't look at me, probably. You know Mary?"

"I've met her."

"That was too bad about her brother, huh?"

I nodded.

She sat down on the day bed and pointed at a pull-up chair. I took it and she crossed her legs, showing me much more of her chunky thighs than I cared to see.

"You're big," she said. "You a fighter or something?"

"Nope. I'm a lover. Like Pete."

It was the wrong thing to say. She had already had a few jolts of booze, I now realized, and it had made her combative.

She flushed. "Smart guy, ain't you? Get lippy around Pete and he'll cut you down to size."

"I'd better be careful," I admitted. "Nothing personal, Miss . . . ?"

"Never mind my name. You're not here to see me. For all I know, even Pete doesn't want to see you. I shouldn't have let you in."

"I'm sorry," I said. "I was trying to be funny. I guess I didn't make it."

"O.K., O.K." She uncrossed her legs. "You live around here?"

"In Montevista," I said. "I have forty acres up there, but I've decided to subdivide it. That'll leave me about ten acres around the house, plenty for a single man."

She looked at me suspiciously. "Montevista? You're trying to be funny again, huh? You don't look like money to me."

"I'm the old money," I explained modestly, "the kind that doesn't have to look it. We're beyond all that up where I live."

"Huh!" she said in doubtful scorn. "You don't fool me."

I knew her now, Red Hovde's spiritual sister, one of the great unfooled. I sighed and shrugged and stared at the stone floor.

Almost a minute of silence, and then she said, "Maybe you're a cop. You're snotty enough."

I made no comment.

The defiance was wavering in her dull face now. For all she knew, I might be the LAW. Her voice was softer. "You a cop?"

Footsteps from outside before I could answer, and she rose quickly and went to the door.

She opened it and said with relief, "Welcome home, Pete. Your friend from Montevista is here."

He came in with the fifth of supermarket bourbon and a bag of ice cubes. Big-time spender on Saturday night.

He looked at me scornfully and just as scornfully at his lady friend. "Montevista? He's a two-bit private eye from down south. He couldn't buy a cemetery lot in Montevista."

"Let's not fight," I said easily. "I'm working for Skip, Pete. Skip needs all the help he can get. I've just had a long talk with—" I paused, to look meaningfully at the blonde.

"With who?" he asked.

"I'd rather tell you privately."

He frowned doubtfully.

Then, "Honey, we ought to have something to eat, too." He handed her a bill. "Gino's is right up the block. Get some ham and rolls and some of those kosher pickles."

"Aw, Pete! I thought we were going to eat out."

He looked at her coldly. "Take about ten minutes. O.K.?"

She sniffed. She snatched the money, picked up her purse from the day bed, muttered something that sounded like "Montevista," and stomped out, slamming the door.

Pete hadn't moved. "So? You had a talk with who?"

"With Juanita. And she explained why Skip hasn't an alibi."

"Who thinks he needs one?"

"Be realistic for a few minutes. He's being held, isn't he? And not on a parking ticket. He's being held on suspicion of murder."

"Crap! You think he can be railroaded with his ex-wife still bleeding for him? You think that Christopher money won't spring him? Who do you think is going to pay your hundred a day?"

"I'm not here to argue, Pete," I said patiently. "Juanita co-operated. She told me enough to put her in trouble if she didn't trust me. I'm asking for help, not anything about your private life."

"Maybe you conned her, but you're not conning me. How much did she tell you?"

"All of it, including the source, her father, and her source for the future, her brother. She put herself way out on a limb telling me those things and you act like I'm working for the Federal Bureau of Narcotics."

"Right now you ain't, maybe. But when the chips are down, you guys save your own damned skins. I know your kind."

"Do you?" I asked patiently. "How many private investigators are there in San Valdesto?"

"One's too many," he said. "Beat it, Callahan!"

"All right. Don't drown yourself in that three-dollar booze."

I brushed past him and opened the door. I was just closing it from the other side when I heard him say, "Montevista! Jesus, how dumb can a dame get?"

For some reason, I didn't feel like Sherlock Holmes as I walked slowly to the car. I had caught Pete Chavez at a bad time, with his loins groaning, so to speak. That had seriously limited his spirit of co-operation. As had the dousing I had given him this morning.

But still I should have learned more; a competent operative would have.

Headquarters wasn't far from here and I considered going over to talk with Lund. There was no other lead; Juanita had given me what she knew and Pete Chavez had given me nothing. The police would match what Pete had told me.

The red Porsche was parked not far from the entrance to Headquarters. I decided not to go in right now; I parked about three spaces up the street.

In a few minutes a big man came out of the wide doorway and down the steps to the walk. It was Joseph Farini. I left the car and got to him before he entered his own car.

He said wearily, "I should have stayed in my field. Lund's absolutely no help at all and the chairman of the police commission phoned me this afternoon and read me the riot act."

"About what?"

"About my insolence to some of the officers down here. I certainly lost a lot of hard-won respect in a short time, representing Skip. You learn anything?"

"Nothing I can reveal and nothing that points a finger. Mrs. Lund is with him now, is she?"

He nodded. "What do you mean—nothing you can reveal?"

"Just that. We can't expect any police co-operation, then?"

"Very damned little. As a matter of fact, the way this Vogel talks, if they can't get Lund for murder, they're determined to get him for something else. Is this 'something else' what you're being secretive about?"

"It could be, counselor. Vogel makes it seem personal, doesn't he?"

Farini nodded, looking at me thoughtfully. "Any theories on why that might be?"

"He's a good friend of Jim Ritter's," I said, "and Ritter is in love with June Lund."

"Oh, Lord," he said sadly. "Why did I ever get mixed up in this?"

"Lund's worth saving," I soothed him. "Get a good night's sleep, counselor. Tomorrow might be a brighter day."

He went away, and in a little while June Lund came out and drove away in her Porsche. I put on my warmest smile and went in to try *my* luck with Skip Lund.

≋≋≋≋≋≋≋ *TWELVE* ≋≋≋≋≋≋≋≋≋

THERE WAS A different man at the desk, and though he admitted that he was a Ram fan, he hesitated about letting me speak with my client.

He said, "I'm not trying to be hard-nosed; don't get me wrong. But, hell, Mrs. Lund has been here three times, and then Farini and that Chavez girl. The chief will have a fit if he comes in and finds *you* in there."

"Has he *ever* come in at this time on a Saturday night?"

"Well, no . . ."

"I'll be quiet," I said. "I'm not on this case just for the money, you know. Lund's getting a lousy deal, in my opinion."

I had guessed right on his personal bias; he nodded. He took a breath and said, "Ten minutes. Long enough?"

"Plenty," I agreed. "And thank you very much."

I didn't go into the cell this time; I stood in front of it. Skip Lund was seated on his cot, bent forward, staring gloomily at the floor. He looked up, some hope in his eyes.

"I'm nowhere," I told him. "Juanita has been very frank,

but I can't see a lead there. Pete won't talk at all and he's angry because Juanita did."

He looked worried. "Juanita told you about—about—"

"About your nonprofit venture," I finished for him. "You were a damned fool for getting involved in something like *that.*"

He nodded. "I know it now. At the time, hell—it looked almost noble. But after you told me about Johnny and those high-school kids—" He rubbed the back of his neck. "It's a stinking, lousy mess, isn't it?"

"It is. Maybe your opinion of Johnny Chavez needs re-evaluation. In the light of what you know now, do you think he might have been trying to double-cross Juanita?"

He shrugged. "My mind won't work. You mean Johnny might have tried to make a deal with some of the L.A. boys?"

"Something like that. Have you ever been approached by outsiders?"

He shook his head thoughtfully. "There was one guy— well, it's maybe nothing, a guy I *heard* had L.A. contacts, but that's all. You know—bar talk."

"So a nothing rumor," I agreed. "What else have we? What's his name and why did he approach you?"

"He didn't approach me," Lund said. "He was a pal of Johnny's in high school and just lately Johnny's been seeing a lot of him again. His name is Pablo Chun. That's a cutie of a name, huh? He's half Mexican and half Chinese."

"Do you know where he lives?"

"In Goleta. It's probably a blind alley. He's got a patio-furniture store near the airport. He sells a lot of that rattan stuff and those hemp and grass squares for rugs. It's called Chun's."

"Does he live there, too?"

"Right behind the store, in a little house. I was only there once, but my memory's right on that, I'm sure."

A nothing rumor—and what else did I have? We talked for a few more minutes, but Chun was the only lead he had. There had been no bail set, he told me; he would have to stay in the clink.

It was almost nine o'clock now, and unless Chun kept his store open on Saturday nights the chances were better than even that my trip would be futile. But it was only a few miles and there was nowhere else to go.

Most of the new electronics firms in the neighborhood were out here, as was the San Valdesto airport. It was a ragged town, a victim of badly planned growth except near the university section.

The store called Chun's was closed. The store-wide sign on the roof informed the potential customer that this was the Tri-County headquarters for raffia and rattan, hemp and grass mats, and kindred importations.

I drove past and parked in front of two converted frame cottages that were now the offices of a doctor of osteopathy and a chiropractor. There was a gap between the buildings, and I could see the front door of another—even smaller—cottage in the back lot behind Chun's.

There was a light showing in this rear house.

I left the car and started out along the crushed stone path that led from the service door of the store to the rear house. I had no official authority to come here—but neither could Chief Harris prevent me from asking Chun questions. This was not San Valdesto.

I was two steps past the rear of the store and a good distance from the front door of the cottage when this—this *monster* came quietly out from the shadow of an oleander bush.

The only light was the reflected light from the house, and in that hazy vision the general outline of the beast resembled a dog. It had to be a dog; no domestic cat was this big and very few horses were this small.

He didn't bark; he didn't growl. He stood calmly in my path, both forefeet planted solidly, his nose pointed in the general direction of my throat.

I assumed that he was staring at me. I knew damned well that I was staring at him, waiting for my eyes to adjust, praying that the anxiety welling in me wouldn't emit an odor of fear that would encourage the beast.

"Hi, doggie," I said weakly.

Nothing from him. He stood motionless, and in my growing vision he seemed to be crouched for springing.

I was afraid to turn my back on him; I didn't have the will to go forward. He looked like one of the Eskimo breeds, wide, big-jawed, and heavy.

"Hi," I said again. "Hello!"

He took a tentative step forward.

"Down," I cautioned quietly. "Heel." He couldn't be vicious, I thought. A vicious dog would be tied or penned. The neighbors and the law would see to that.

But it was his yard, not mine.

Now he was crouching. I could see him clearly and I listened for the warning growl above the pounding of my heart. Maybe he only wanted to play, I told myself skeptically. Maybe he was crouching for a playful leap.

At my jugular.

If he would only make some sound. If he would growl or snarl or wag his tail—anything but crouch there silently, making me sweat.

I took the chance and shouted, "Hey, Chun! Your dog's loose!"

It prompted him into action. He leaped and I side-stepped frenziedly. One of his huge paws scraped my forearm.

"Down, damn you!" I shouted at the top of my lungs while I covered my face with my arms.

The light flashed on in the yard and a voice from the direction of the house shouted, "Kong, come here!" And, in a quieter voice, "Don't panic, mister. He only wants to play. He wouldn't hurt a fly."

I lowered my arms from in front of my face and explained with dignity, "I'm not a fly. What the hell is he?"

"An Alaskan Malemute. Sled dog. Lousy watchdog. Too friendly." A pause. "And who are you?"

"My name is Callahan. Are you Pablo Chun?"

"I'm not Picasso," he said wryly. "You selling something?"

"Nothing. I came for information."

A pause, and then, "What kind of information?"

"Information about the death of Johnny Chavez."

A longer pause. His dog was at his side now, his attention still on me. I couldn't see Chun's face. I saw only his outline. He was tall and heavy with a rounded look, slope-shouldered, thick-armed, his head big on a thick neck.

The silence grew and I said, "I'm a private detective hired by Skip Lund."

A continuation of the silence for perhaps half a minute. Then he said dully, "All right. Come on in. I can't help you, though."

I came up the two steps that led to his front door and into a small living room furnished in mail-order *moderne*. Pablo Chun pointed to a square, stuffed chair and I sat in it.

He continued to stand, facing me. He had a round face, dark and strong, with only a suggestion of oriental cast to his brown eyes.

He said, "Back in high school, I used to know Johnny. We played basketball together. We haven't been close since."

"I understand you've been seeing him more than usual lately."

"Who told you that?"

"I think it was a police officer," I lied.

His dog came over to lay his massive head on my knee. I rubbed the coarse fur of his neck and scratched him behind the ears. He slobbered on my knee.

"Kong!" Chun said sharply. He pointed toward a corner of the room. "Down!"

The beast went slowly over to lie in the corner, his eyes reminiscently on me.

Chun said doubtfully, "If the police told you that, why haven't they been to see me?"

"I don't know."

"You lied, didn't you?"

"I can't reveal the officer's name," I lied further, "but he told me that. Isn't it true?"

"It might be. It has no meaning, though."

I said, "He's been eating without working. How did he do that?"

Chun shrugged.

"He sat ninety days on a reefer rap," I went on doggedly. "Maybe he graduated to the Big H."

From the direction of the airport came the sound of a plane revving before take-off. Kong's ears lifted and he turned to stare in the direction of the sound.

Chun said, "You're fishing. I don't know what Johnny's business was."

"You haven't even an informed guess?"

Chun was growing annoyed. He asked, "Why are you bothering me? You figure because I'm half Chinese I'm bound to be in the opium racket or something?"

"Nothing like that," I said soothingly. "You were right before; I'm fishing. I have a little information and I need a lot more. I'm not accusing you of any complicity."

There was emotion in his voice. "If I knew who killed Johnny Chavez, the police would have the killer's name. I'm a businessman, Mr. Callahan. My books are open. What Johnny did was his business. What I do is sell raffia and rattan and garden furniture."

The plane had warmed up now, and its thunder grew as it gained momentum down the runway. Kong's head lifted as the sound rose; he was still staring into space when there was only a distant drone.

I stood up. "It looks like I was given a bum lead. I apologize, Mr. Chun, for bothering you this time of night."

His voice was calmer now. "No trouble." He sighed. "Johnny was always in hot water one way or another. If it wasn't money, it was women. A lot of people didn't like Johnny Chavez."

He came to the door with me as I went out into a night that had turned noticeably colder in the short time I had been inside.

The car's engine was still warm; the heater gave me almost instant heat. Nowhere, nowhere, nowhere. . . .

I am quite often disturbed by my own sense of insufficiency, but tonight was a new low. Chun, Lund, Chavez — none of them had given me even a ghost of a lead. Juanita had been frank, but I had almost guessed what she had told me.

Nothing, nothing, nothing, nowhere. . . . I drove back to the motel in a real ugly mood.

And there behind my rear door the green Pontiac station wagon was parked. James Edward Ritter started to climb out of it as soon as he recognized my car. He was drunk.

That much was clear as he walked carefully toward me. He was drunk and I had to assume that he was going to be belligerent. I could only hope that he wouldn't cause enough of a fuss to bring the police.

He stopped walking about three feet from me as I stood next to my car.

He said raspingly, "You son-of-a-bitch!"

"Slow down," I warned him. "It's been a bad day. What's your beef, Ritter?"

"You," he said. "Put up your hands, you bastard."

"Come inside and talk quietly," I said, "or I'll send for the police."

"You'll send for the police? You haven't got any friends in this town Callahan. Now put up your hands or crawl into your hole."

I turned and started for the manager's office and he moved quickly to put a hand on my shoulder and turn me around.

He had turned me with his left hand and his right was cocked for delivery. I suppose I could have moved inside of it and wrestled him to some kind of sanity, but the day had held too many frustrations.

I moved inside of his wild right, pushed him back, and threw a right of my own, a punch that carried the added weight of the day's humiliations.

It was on target; he went down and out, as cold as the night.

≋≋≋≋≋≋≋ *THIRTEEN* ≋≋≋≋≋≋≋

ON THE BED he stirred and moaned and then sat up as I came from the bathroom with a cold, wet washrag.

"How the hell did I get here?" he asked.

"I carried you. You all right?"

He swung his feet around and then thought better of it as a wave of dizziness must have hit him. "Carried me?" he mumbled sickly. "I weigh over two hundred pounds."

"I noticed that. You're not going to vomit, are you?"

He stared at me in sick indignation. "I haven't done *that*, Callahan, since I left high school."

Small prides for petty men. . . . I said, "Would you like some coffee?"

"I don't want *anything* of yours," he said. "You and I will go around again, Callahan, when I'm sober."

"Any time," I assured him. "I like you, too."

He felt his jaw gingerly and tried once more to swing his feet around to the floor. This time he made it and sat on the edge of the bed, his head forward, his hands pressing down hard on the rough-textured spread.

He said quietly, "You think you can do Lund some good?

He's dead. He's going to jail, whether he killed Chavez or not. That's the way it's going to be and you may as well go home right now."

I said, "If that's the way it's going to be, why did you come over here tonight?"

"Because until you came up here, June was through with that bum. Today she couldn't stay away from him." He lifted his head to glare at me. "He's a bum and his friends are rats."

"And you love his wife," I said. "There are always complications, Ritter, when you mess with another man's wife."

"Mess?" he said. "Watch your language." He rubbed his neck. "I love her. We're going to be married."

I said nothing.

His voice quieter, he said, "Who's paying you? And how much?"

"My client's paying me the standard rate, a hundred a day."

A silence, and then, "How many miles do you get on a gallon in that jalopy of yours?"

"About fifteen. Why?"

He stared at me levelly. "I was wondering how far away a thousand dollars would take you."

"It wouldn't get me out of town," I told him. "I'm for rent, Ritter, but never for sale. I think you'd better leave now."

He stood up shakily. "You figure you and Lund can get into June's money? She took care of that a month ago. I'll give you twelve hundred."

"Good night," I said. "Be smart. Leave now."

"I'm going." He felt his jaw once more and stretched his neck. "And if you're smart, you'll leave now, too. You've been warned."

"Good night," I said.

He went out and slammed the door. In a minute I heard the sound of his tires squealing on black-top as he gunned away. He, too, hadn't told me anything I hadn't guessed. If they couldn't get Skip for murder, they felt, down at Headquarters, that they could put him away on a narcotics charge.

Juanita must have known that, but she hadn't seemed worried.

High-school buddies, Vogel and Ritter, Chun and Chavez. Old loyalties, well-intrenched bigotries—and I scratched at the surface of nothing, a futile quest in an insular town. Why didn't I quit?

This is Don Boyer, Brock. This is Brock Callahan, Don. Who'd want me?

I undressed slowly, trying to think, to find a thread or a pattern, a forgotten aside or a telling slip of the tongue. Nothing. I showered for a long time, hoping to wash out with drumming water the tight knot between my shoulder blades.

In about an hour I fell asleep. And dreamed of a girl I'd known years ago in my high-school English class.

Sunday morning dawned hot and clear. At the pancake restaurant I bought a copy of the Los Angeles *Times* and dawdled over my coffee as I skimmed it. Though I malign the paper constantly, I cannot live for long without it.

It covered in its thorough way this murder up here, and in this Sunday edition it included a résumé of the case up to now. There was nothing in the account I didn't know, but I read it carefully, hoping to find in the printed summary some pattern that hadn't shown in my day-to-day questioning.

Nothing.

The waitress was patiently pouring me my third cup of

coffee when I saw the dark-skinned policeman enter, still in civvies, as he had been last night.

He stood in the doorway and then headed directly for my small table.

When he was standing before me, I said, "Good morning, officer. Sit down and have a free cup of coffee."

"Thank you," he said softly, and sat in the chair across from me. "My name is Juan Montegro. I started my vacation last night but have decided to stay in town a few days."

"Because of what's happened?"

He nodded. He licked his lower lip. "Juanita was—indiscreet last night."

"She trusts me. Did you know what was going on?"

A pause, and then he nodded.

"Does Sergeant Vogel, too?" I guessed.

A longer pause and another nod.

"And who else?" I asked.

"A man named Captain Dahl. Have you met him?"

"No. Why are you telling me this?"

"Because Lund did not kill Chavez. Because Sergeant Vogel is being a bad police officer due to his friendship with James Ritter." He licked his lower lip again. "I thought you might need some ammunition later."

"Ammunition? You mean my knowing that Dahl and Vogel let this illegal operation continue? You *can't* mean I should blackmail them with it?"

His dark face stiffened. "Of course not! I thought of it as a lever, as a shield."

"And you'd back me up?"

"I would support you with documentation without the necessity of identifying myself. I like my job, Mr. Callahan."

"I don't get your angle," I said. "No offense, now."

"Justice," he said. "Is that an angle? We know Skip was on that boat, hundreds of miles from where Chavez died. We seem to be the only men who are concerned about his innocence."

He sipped his coffee and I sipped mine. I asked, "Does Chief Harris know what's going on?"

"He doesn't want to know about this. No new narcotic cases in the district, a forty per cent decrease in robberies and prostitution—he is happy with the result without wanting to know the reason."

"And that's why you let it continue?" I said. "You and Vogel and this Captain Dahl?"

He nodded. "Don't judge us too harshly. We kept an eye on it; it would end when it stopped doing good."

Another hunch came to me and I said, "Were you *told* to take your vacation now?"

He smiled. "Nothing of the kind. I picked this time last January."

"Do you know who killed Chavez?"

He shook his head. "Was Chun any help?"

I stared at him.

"Vogel knows you went there last night," he explained. "But Chun's clean. He's been checked very carefully by the Department, and he was spotless."

"Why was he checked?"

"Because of his mother. She lives down south with her new husband."

"His mother?"

"Her new husband," Montegro said, "is Carmine Licussa."

A name. Kefauver's committee had considered Licussa a don in the Maffia. Impossible to prove, but every citizen over twelve knew he was a hoodlum and a millionaire.

"Licussa," I said wonderingly. "That *is* the majors."

"He tried to buy a home up here," Juan Montegro said. "In Slope Ranch. He was turned down."

I said nothing, thinking the obvious. If Johnny wanted to go out on his own, back on the trail of the big buck, he would need a new source. And what better source than his old buddy, now a stepson of the great Carmine Licussa?

Officer Juan Montegro said, "You're nowhere, aren't you?"

I nodded.

"So are we," he said, "if that's any consolation. Our first thought was like yours—some Syndicate gun from down south that Chavez was dealing with. None of it is checking out."

"So what chance have I in a strange town?"

He sighed. "None, probably. But I hope you will continue. I followed your work on that Mary Mae Milgrim case. That solution came out of left field, and you seem to have an instinct for those." He stood up. "I will stay in town for a few days. I am in the phone book. Thanks for the coffee."

He went out. I finished my coffee and went out two minutes later.

An *instinct*, he had said. Lacking intelligence, what else can a man work on? An instinct. It is not always the answers to questions that are revealing, not always the things that are said. It is often the things that are not said or the things said that don't seem important—what actors call the throwaway lines.

But none of them was pointing a finger this hot Sunday morning. I had no place to go; I went back to the motel.

I'd had a call, the manager told me. A Miss Christopher. I called her back.

"You don't work on Sundays, do you?" she asked. "I thought you could come for dinner. About two?"

"I'd work," I said, "if I had anything to work on. I'm stymied, Glenys."

A silence, and then, "I heard something yesterday that disturbs me very much—that Skip was involved in transporting narcotics."

"Don't believe everything you hear. Bud wasn't around when you heard it, was he?"

"No. But he'll hear it, won't he, eventually? This is a small town, Brock."

"I'm well aware of that. And who told you?"

Another silence, and then, "Jim Ritter."

"Was he sober?"

"Of course. Now what does *that* mean?"

"He was drunk when he attacked me last night. He was waiting for me when I got back to the motel. He tried to bribe me after the attack failed."

"Brock . . . ? This isn't—you're not—*is that the truth?*"

"I swear it. About the dinner, if I don't call you before one, I'll be there at two. I may find something worth investigating, but I doubt it. Chin up."

"You, too," she said. "I'll be waiting."

Waiting? Glenys Christopher? For me? Oh, no, we must put an end to that. I had a girl. I went to my room to see if there was a bottle of Einlicher left.

There was one bottle, and I was opening it when someone knocked at my door.

It was Sergeant Bernard Vogel.

"Come in, Sergeant," I said civilly. "This is the last bottle of beer, but I can get you a Coke out of the machine in the playroom."

"No, thanks," he said. He came in and I closed the door against the day's heat.

I took a swig of beer, waiting.

He said heavily, "A man named Pablo Chun phoned Headquarters last night and wanted to know why you were questioning him. So do I."

"Why should he phone your Department? He's not in San Valdesto municipal jurisdiction, is he?"

Vogel colored.

"I haven't been warned by the sheriff. Chief Harris said he was going to phone him."

He stared at me, his face still flushed.

I said quietly, "I went to see Pablo Chun because he was a stepson of Carmine Licussa's. I had a hunch, not proven out, that Johnny Chavez was friendly with Chun *because* he was a stepson of the great Licussa."

"And what did you learn?"

"Nothing. But, while you're here, I'd like to ask a question."

He waited, saying nothing.

I said, "Your friend Ritter was waiting for me last night, drunk, belligerent. When his belligerence failed to frighten me, he tried to bribe me. I'm not putting in a complaint because I know he's a friend of yours. But, in return for that favor, I'd like to know who told him that Skip Lund was involved in the narcotics traffic?"

Vogel was breathing heavily, glaring, speechless.

I waited, sipping my beer.

Finally, he managed, "You skate on thin ice."

"I get paid for it. Ritter told Miss Christopher that. If Bud Lund hears it, because of Ritter, I'm warning you right now, Sergeant, that I'm going after your friend. And you'll need more cops than you have in this town to stop me."

His voice was a dead monotone. "I think you'd better come downtown with me right now."

"Fair enough. Do the reporters in this hamlet work on Sunday?"

Some wariness in his anger now, some doubt in his glare.

I said quietly, "I'm sure I have a story of great local interest for any reporter."

More doubt.

And I added, "Involving Department complicity in a rather unique local operation."

He said hoarsely, "You son-of-a-bitch!"

"I don't like to work this way, Sergeant. But I have to function in order to eat. And I intend to eat."

"You're bluffing," he said.

"It's possible," I admitted. "Are you calling the bluff?"

He gave it a lot of thought. He gave it enough thought to worry me, because my threat to call in a reporter would also reveal the shame of his father to Bud Lund.

Finally, he said, "I won't call your bluff today. I'll repeat the chief's warning to you—*stay out of our business!*"

I had won my point; I could afford to look humble and I did.

And then he diminished my hole card by saying, "If we have to, we'll run you in and you can call all the reporters in town. Just remember that Bud Lund is old enough to read."

I had nothing to say. He had made my present edge momentary and precarious; he had reduced my ace to a jack. But he hadn't called me, and I could guess why. He was a friend of Ritter's; he knew that I was a friend of at least *one* Christopher. Where the big money was involved, Sergeant Vogel would move warily.

He went out and I looked longingly at the pool. Jan had sent my trunks up with Glenys. I had no place to go with further questions; I was at a dead end.

I didn't go out. I sat in the room and put all their names down on paper. I connected them with their lines of interest, delineated their peeves, their hates, their hopes, seeking the elusive.

All blanks. Officer Juan Montegro had said that I had

come at the Mary Mae Milgrim solution from left field, but that solution had been intrinsic in the relationship of the principals in the case.

A man can be hit by a speeding car on his way to a bank robbery and the bank robbery will have nothing to do with the man's death. Narcotics didn't *have* to be involved in the death of Johnny Chavez.

We weren't even sure at this time that Chavez had been murdered. It could have been an accident, a stray bullet from another hunter's gun.

Out at the pool the tourists frolicked and laughed and splashed and sunned themselves. In my room I sat in the doldrums of a loser. What could I tell Bud if I went up there for dinner?

The possibility of Pete Chavez as an alibi for Johnny was weak on two counts: the police distrust of Chavez and Pete's own reluctance to stick his neck out by admitting something that at least three officers in the Department already knew.

The ammunition that Montegro had given me was not the kind I liked to use. Around Los Angeles I worked *with* the police. And around the Los Angeles area this kind of ammunition wasn't available.

At one o'clock I took a quick dip in the pool. At two o'clock I was turning into the driveway of the Lund home in Montevista.

Glenys was in the open doorway when I came up from the parking area. "Two o'clock means two o'clock to you, doesn't it? We haven't even started the charcoal."

"The lower classes are always punctual," I said. "How is Bud holding up today?"

"He seems to be all right. He's over at a neighbor's." She smiled. "He has a lot of faith in you."

We were in the living room now, and June was sitting on the same sofa where she had spilled the drink. She was leafing through a copy of *Vogue*.

"Hi, halfback," she said casually. "My sister's been keeping the Einlicher cold for you all morning."

I turned to see the beginning of a blush on Glenys' tanned cheeks.

"Nonsense," she said. "Would you like something, June?" She was walking toward the liquor cabinet.

"Nothing," June said. "I think I'll give the booze a little vacation."

Glenys' eyebrows lifted, but she made no comment. She brought me a bottle of beer and asked, "How are you with charcoal? The housekeeper is off today."

"There's an electric lighter around somewhere," June said. "I'll start the fire." She stood up and went out.

Glenys poured Martini into a fairly large glass and loaded it with ice cubes. She said quietly, "I think the housekeeper's been fired. What's going on with Skip and my sister?"

"I didn't know anything was. How do you mean?"

"I think they're going back together again. I heard that Skip might even get back into the gas-station business." She paused. "If he *ever* gets out of jail."

"Would that make you unhappy?"

"Not for a minute. They are both adults. I have stopped being Aunt Glenys."

I smiled at her. "By request?"

She glared at me quietly.

I sipped the fine beer, ignoring her glare.

"All right!" she said finally. "I was told off. I was called stuffy and class-conscious."

"By June?"

Glenys sniffed and nodded.

I said, "It's *her* life. I don't think you're stuffy. And if I had your money, I'd be class-conscious as all get-out. Why have it if you can't enjoy it?"

"I'm sane," she said. "Sane, sane, *sane!* In my family, that's a vice."

She took a healthy gulp of her Martini. "That Mary Chavez is going to be surprised, I'll bet, if June and Skip get together again."

"And hurt," I said. "She loves him."

"He'll never get out of jail," she said, after a few seconds. "He was born to wind up in jail, that man."

"You could be right. But he's not your problem."

And then Bud was standing in the archway from the entry hall and I wondered if he had heard his aunt's prophecy.

"Hi," he said, and looked at me questioningly.

"Good afternoon," I said. "Nothing new, Bud. It's not an easy case. They never are until they're over. You keep your chin up."

"Sure," he said. "Who's Mary Chavez, Brock?"

Glenys looked startled. I said calmly, "She's the sister of the man who was killed. Where did you hear her name?"

"Mr. Ritter and Mom were arguing last night," he said, "and he said Mary Chavez was a little tramp and Pop was crazy for her." He looked at me levelly. "Is that true?"

"No," I said. "Mr. Ritter, Bud, has a big mouth and a small brain. You've got to believe in your dad, just as I do."

Glenys went to pour some more Martini over the ice cubes in her glass. Bud stared at me doubtfully. "Dad *was* doing secret work, wasn't he?"

"Yes," I said. "Work he thought important and helpful to sick people."

He seemed to be digesting that. Then he asked, "Where's Mom?"

"On the patio," his aunt told him, "getting the fire started. Steak today, boy."

He went out and Glenys looked accusingly at me. "Jim was right then? Narcotics?"

"I explained about Ritter to Bud," I said, "and I thought you were listening. He has a big mouth and a bird brain and I am glad I cooled him last night. Let's stay off that topic; the thought of that freak spoils my day."

"Well!" she said. "Aren't you worked up? And why?"

"Frustration," I said wearily, "and ugly-minded people. Is there another beer handy?"

She took a bottle out of the ice chest. "Narcotics. And June making plans. He will stay in jail, won't he? He hasn't a chance of getting out, and I think it's cruel to keep Bud's hopes up."

"He has a chance," I said. "It's too complicated for me to explain, but Ritter's good friend, Sergeant Vogel, is not working with clean hands himself. I repeat — it's complicated and *not really any of your business, Glenys.*"

A miffed silence from her, and I said more calmly, "I'm sorry. I'm not permitted to tell you anything about it; it was told to me in confidence. I shouldn't have told you about Vogel."

This was not the bedroom Glenys I was talking with; this was the matriarch. Some strain settled in the room and carried over to the later steaks on the patio. June tried to be chipper, and the non-alcoholic June was a naturally cheerful girl.

Despite June, the meal was as uncomfortable as the first meal I had eaten in this house. Bud was quiet and abstracted, Glenys disturbed by the thought of June's getting once more emotionally involved with the hot-rodder.

I had more reason than June to be cheerful; I wasn't as involved with Lund as she was. But I was more involved with the realities of life than she was and I didn't share her optimism about his eventual and certain release.

Her view of the law was conditioned by her background. Where she had grown up, in Beverly Hills in one of the *big* houses, the law had been politely on her side since birth.

My view of it was closer to Skip's—the poor man's view, a more pessimistic prism.

Well, he still had Farini. And, of course, Callahan.

The phone rang and everybody sat and then June must have realized that there were no servants in the house. She went to answer it.

She came back to tell me that the call was for me—a Captain Dahl.

It was the name Officer Montegro had mentioned, the third party in the triumvirate aware of Juanita's transportation service.

He said, "They told me at the motel where you could be reached. I guess you know where Lund's apartment is, don't you?"

"Yes," I said. "Is that where you are?"

"That's where I am," he said, "and I'd like to see you here."

"What's happened, Captain?"

"Pete Chavez has been murdered," he said.

≋≋≋≋≋ *FOURTEEN* ≋≋≋≋≋

DRIVING INTO TOWN, I reflected that the murder of Pete Chavez, with Skip in jail, could indicate to some minds that Skip was now less likely to be guilty of the original Chavez murder. But the police mind is not that gullible. All it would prove to the police was that Skip was not guilty of killing Pete.

And why had Dahl phone me? Perhaps someone had told the police that I'd talked with Pete last night—but what someone? A neighbor wouldn't be that nosy. If the S.V.P.D. had learned it by following me, Ritter would have mentioned it this morning, I was sure. Perhaps Pete had beefed to Skip about my visit and Skip had told the police or they had overheard.

There were two Department cars parked in front of the adobe apartment building, and a knot of buzzing citizens clustered on the sidewalk, under the bottle-brush tree. I pushed my way through these inquisitive taxpayers to the covered, ground-level porch that served all four units.

A uniformed officer was guarding the door to Skip's apartment. I told him, "Captain Dahl sent for me. Would you tell him I'm here? My name is Callahan."

The man pointed to a tall, thin man in a gray suit standing next to a covered body. He moved aside to let me in.

Captain Dahl had high cheekbones, freckles, and eyes of an extremely vivid blue.

"Callahan?" he asked, and I nodded.

A momentary silence, which I filled. "Not another .30-.30, I suppose. This was a city kill."

"He was stabbed," Dahl said. "What was your beef with him?"

I frowned. "Beef? None."

His voice was harsh. "You threw him off the pier, didn't you?"

I remembered the counterman and his glasses. Had he reported this? I said, "Yes. In self-protection. I bore him no grudge."

"When was the last time you saw him?"

"About seven o'clock last night."

There was interest now in the bright-blue eyes; it almost looked like hope. He asked quietly, "Was he alone?"

I killed the hope by saying, "No. There was a girl with him."

"What was her name?"

"I don't know, Captain. I wasn't introduced."

He stared at me skeptically.

I said, "I'm sure she lives in town. He sent her to some place he called Gino's for ham and rolls and pickles. It's in the neighborhood. Maybe they know her."

"We'll check that," he said. "Hang around." He went over to talk with the man at the door.

The uniformed man left and Sergeant Bernard Vogel came in. He didn't seem surprised to see me. Behind him came the boys with the wheeled stretcher.

The body was lifted and taken out while Vogel and Dahl

talked together near the door to the bathroom. Occasionally they glanced my way, and I had the uncomfortable feeling that they were discussing me. My hole card was now about a seven or eight.

Vogel went out again and Dahl came over to tell me, "We'll go down to the station and wait for Vogel to check out your alibi."

"Alibi?" I could feel my hackles rise. "Alibi? That was a strange choice of words, Captain. Am I being charged with something?"

"Not yet," he said lightly. "If this Gino, or whatever his name is, can name the girl and she corroborates your story, well—"

"You'll think of something else," I finished for him. "I don't like any of this, Captain."

"I wouldn't either," he said, "if I were in your shoes. Let's go. We'll take your car."

A number of hot words came to my mind, but I voiced none of them. We went meekly out to my car, through the dispersing crowd.

"Don't sulk," Dahl told me in the car. "We have to have you fingerprinted, don't we? We lifted a good one in the room."

"You must have found a hundred of them," I said. "What does that prove?"

"The *good* one," he said, "was in blood."

I carefully controlled the tone of my voice. "And you are suggesting that the bloody fingerprint *could be mine?*"

"I'm sure it isn't mine," he said in his casual and superior way. "Are you suggesting that we haven't a right to take the print of a man who admits being there last night?"

"I think it constitutes harrassment," I said, "and I here and now request permission to phone my attorney, Joseph Farini, as soon as we get to a phone."

"Permission granted," he said. "We'll take the prints first."

They took the prints and I phoned Farini at his home. There was no answer. I thought of calling Glenys but decided to wait until Vogel came in after questioning the people at Gino's.

In the small room off the front hall I waited for Vogel and his report. Johnny Chavez and now Pete. . . . Was Juanita losing her army? Or had Pete been the victim of a *personal* enemy, a man who had some reason to hate the Chavez family? I thought of Mary and hoped that this last was not the answer.

I had been in the small and unoccupied room for about fifteen minutes when Vogel came in with the officer who had been guarding the door to Lund's apartment.

Vogel said, "No luck at Gino's. Come with us."

We went into the chief's office. Harris wasn't there. Captain Dahl sat behind his desk and Skip Lund sat in a chair nearby. Vogel pointed out a chair for me and took one himself. The other officer said something quietly to Dahl and then went out.

Skip asked me, "Is it true—about Pete?"

I nodded.

Dahl said to me, "I'd like a physical description of this girl you saw in the apartment last night and any other facts about her that might help identify her."

I gave him a physical description. I thought of her mentioning that she knew Mary Chavez and decided not to repeat that. Mary had already had enough trouble with Vogel. I did tell him that the girl admired Skip.

Dahl looked at Skip. "You know the girl, then?"

Skip was pale and obviously shaken by the news of Pete's death. He licked his lips and said hoarsely, "I met a girl who looked like that. I only met her once. She was with

Pete. I don't remember her name."

"Where did you meet her?" Dahl asked.

"In front of the First Security Bank on Rodeo Street."

Dahl said acidly, "That's a big help. If we find out you're lying, Lund—"

"What will you do?" Skip asked. "Put me in jail?"

It was a bitter comment. But I had to smile.

Vogel said sharply, "What's so goddamned funny, Callahan?"

Anger bubbled in me. I shrugged.

"You're just asking for lumps," Vogel went on.

I shook my head. "I'm getting them. Spiritual lumps. You boys have been destroying my ego. I think you'd better lock me up before I belt somebody."

Captain Dahl looked perplexedly at Vogel and coolly at me. "If there's a rational explanation for that last remark, could we have it?"

"You're new to the Vogel-Lund-Ritter-Callahan relationship, Captain," I told him calmly. "None of it has anything to do with efficient police investigation."

He was frowning now and he glanced at Vogel. I thought Vogel colored. I knew he glared at me.

Dahl asked me quietly, "Why was the name Ritter brought into this?"

"He was a high-school buddy of Sergeant Vogel's," I explained. "He and the sergeant have maintained the friendship through the years, and when Ritter fell in love with Mrs. Lund the two of them must have decided to get Skip out of the way."

Vogel was up out of his chair immediately and facing me. "Get on your feet, you bastard! Nobody talks that way about me."

"Sit down," I told him calmly. "I'm not armed, but I'm sure if I started on you, I'd kill you with my hands. And too many have died already. Now sit down or I will get up."

He reached a hand for my neck—and Dahl said, "Sergeant, sit down!"

Vogel drew back his hand, glaring at me, breathing heavily.

"Sit down or turn in your badge," Dahl said. "Right now!"

"Or give the captain your gun," I suggested, "and you and I will go into that room down the hall. The boys can make bets on who comes out."

Dahl said gratingly, "Callahan, watch it! That's the last warning."

I took a deep breath and slumped in my chair. I didn't look at anybody. "I'd like to phone Mr. Farini again." I paused. "Or another attorney, if he's not available."

Dahl's voice was softer. "Simmer down. You're not being charged with anything yet." To Vogel, he said, "Sit down, Bernie."

Vogel sat down. Lund stirred in his chair and coughed quietly. Dahl looked doubtfully at me. "I've heard that you threatened Sergeant Vogel this morning with police complicity in something illegal. Are you ready to document that now?"

I met his doubtful gaze. "If you'll give me two hours. I don't like to do it unless I'm forced to, however. I'm not here to cause trouble. My sole business in this town is finding the murderer of Johnny Chavez. I had expected police co-operation in that. I was told not to investigate it by Sergeant Vogel."

"And Chief Harris," Vogel added.

Dahl looked at Vogel and I could guess that he was remembering that Chief Harris didn't know what Dahl and Vogel (and Juan Montegro) knew about Johnny Chavez.

A silence.

I asked, "Haven't my fingerprints been checked against the bloody one yet?"

Dahl nodded. "You're clear there."

"Thank you," I said dryly. "I was worried."

Dahl glanced coolly at me and looked again at Vogel. "Bernie, Mr. Callahan has a very solid reputation down south."

"So I've heard," Vogel said. And added, "From him. It's your decision, Captain. I don't think we should call the chief in on this."

Captain Dahl's bright-blue eyes moved from Vogel to Lund and then to me. "Do you think you might be able to find that girl who was with Chavez last night?"

"I might. With your permission, I'll try."

"Go," he said wearily. "Try."

I stood up. "How about my client? Doesn't tonight's murder clear him of the other?"

Vogel muttered. Dahl looked at me and smiled.

I smiled back at him. "O.K., Captain. You can't blame a man for trying even the absurd. I'll keep in touch." I winked at Skip. "Chin up."

He smiled and gestured weakly.

Outside, I stood for a minute looking at the Sunday traffic, sparse and leisurely traffic. Where would I start? Where but the hub of the web? I climbed into the hot flivver and headed for Chickie's.

There were two couples at two tables and one couple at the bar. The guitar player was sitting on a straight chair in a corner, drinking a glass of wine. His guitar leaned against the wall next to him.

"Pancho!" Juanita greeted me. "And what's new?"

I said, "Bad news. Pete Chavez has been killed."

Her hand gripped the bar and she stared at me in shock.

"Stabbed to death," I said, "in Skip Lund's apartment."

Her full bosom rose and fell. "No—*no!*"

The couple at the bar glanced our way.

"Yes," I said quietly. "Is there someplace where we could talk more privately?"

She nodded toward the small table we had shared before. She said something in Spanish to the guitar player and he finished his wine and came over to stand behind the bar as we went over to the corner table.

There, when we were seated, I said, "It has to be connected with your business now. First Johnny and then Pete. What other connection could there be?"

"No," she whispered. "No! That's not true."

"An outsider," I guessed, "getting rid of your team, one by one."

She shook her head emphatically. "There is no reason to think like that. I have talked with Pablo Chun. His stepfather has no interest in this town, except to live here, if the police will let him."

The thin bartender with the scar came in from the kitchen and went behind the bar. The guitar player went back to his chair and picked up his instrument.

Juanita said, "You will be looking now for the one who killed Pete. You will learn it has nothing to do with our trade."

"How can you be sure? Do you know something you're not telling me, Juanita?"

She shook her head. Her brown eyes welled with tears and she rubbed them with the back of a hand. "Pete," she murmured. "Peter, Peter . . . who, who, *who?*"

"I don't know. The police have asked me to find the girl who was with him last night. I promised them I'd try."

"You? You working with the police?"

"Every time they'll let me," I said. "I told you that the first night. A few of them down at Headquarters know about you and your little charity, don't they?"

"Not much. They might suspect, but they don't want to *know*. When did you get so friendly with the police?"

I didn't answer.

She called out in Spanish to the bartender and he nodded and poured a tall glass of beer. He brought it to the table and set it in front of me as the guitar began to send sad music through the room.

"Thank you," I said to the bartender. I looked at Juanita. "Do you know who the girl was?"

She didn't answer me, staring gloomily into space.

"A chunky, blond girl," I said. "She knows Mary Chavez and she knows Skip. Skip couldn't identify her and I didn't tell the police about Mary. I figured Mary had been bothered enough already by the miserable Vogel."

Some interest in her sad eyes. "I thought you were working for them."

"*With* them," I said; "not *for* them. My work is private and if they don't respect that privacy, I don't even work *with* them."

The guitar went from the sweet sadness to the pure sirup and I sipped my beer.

"You will protect me?" Juanita said. "You have no reason not to protect me."

"Protect you how?"

"If I find out the name of this girl, you will not tell the police where you learned it?"

"I can promise that."

She stood up and looked down at me for a few seconds. Then she turned and walked through the swinging door that led to the kitchen.

She was quite a woman, growing more attractive in my

154 *William Campbell Gault*

mind as I knew her better. If I had met her in my less
sophisticated youth, there was a possibility that I would be
behind that bar tonight. I knew she could cook; I had tasted
her food. Even a bigoted slob like Lars Hovde was not
immune to her charms.

The guitar followed my mood, sensual and ruminative,
and I turned to study this psychic strummer. His long, thin
face acknowledged nothing, his bony fingers plucked on,
his expression as empty as the wine glass on the floor next
to his chair.

Juanita came back and handed me a slip of paper. "The
name and address are there. Remember now . . ." She put
a finger in front of her pursed lips.

"I promise." I stood up. "Juanita, this is the end of your
misguided charity. You can't hush up a murder."

"The murderer will be found," she said confidently, "and
everything will go on as before."

What was it to me? It wasn't even my town. We stood
gazing at each other while the guitar strummed softly. Sweet
music and the big H, mantillas and murder.

"You go see that girl," she urged, "that—anglo."

I sighed and argued no more. She was the queen and we
lived in a matriarchate. I nodded a good night and went out
to look up the imitation blonde.

~~~~~~~~~~ *FIFTEEN* ~~~~~~~~~~

HER NAME WAS Rita Wollard and she lived in the north end of town, a section given over to new tract housing and stucco apartment buildings, a raw area alien to the older parts of town.

It was a little after eight now and a Sunday night. She might have a date, though I doubted it. How many men in this town could be as hungry as Pete Chavez had obviously been?

On one of the stucco apartment buildings her name was paired with another on a mailbox. The other name was Helen Garden, and the apartment was listed as Number 23.

I went up the outside stairs to a roofed runway that served the second-floor apartments. Their apartment was on the end, with an unobstructed view of the supermarket parking lot.

I could hear voices through the door, a man's voice and a woman's. The woman's voice didn't sound like Rita's, as I remembered it. I rang the bell.

Rita opened the door and the odor of cheap perfume

drifted out. "Jesus!" she said. "The Montevista hot-shot. Now what, muscles?"

"I'd like to speak with you," I said. "Pete Chavez has been killed."

Her mouth opened and her stocky body stiffened. She stared in silence.

From behind her, a man's voice said, "If it's a guy, grab him, Rita. It's too late to be fussy now."

A woman laughed.

Rita continued to stare at me. Finally, in a whisper, "How was he killed? His car?"

"He was stabbed," I said.

She was breathing heavily. "What have I got to do with it? Why are you here?"

"You were with him last night. The police will want to talk with you."

She looked back over her shoulder and then at me again. Her voice was anxious. "Do they have to know? They're going out for dinner now. They'll be gone in a couple minutes."

"Shall I wait downstairs?"

"No. Come in. But don't say nothing about Pete. These people here—well, they're not crazy for Mexicans."

I went into a new apartment furnished in what looked like castoffs. Rita's cellmate, Helen Garden, was a tall, thin girl with imitation red hair.

Her date for the evening was named Al Dunkert, a tanned and lanky man with an amiable grin and nasal voice. Why didn't we join them for dinner? he wanted to know.

I told him I had eaten my dinner.

He smiled knowingly. "I get you. Maybe we can pick you up after dinner, huh? How much time you need?"

Rita flushed. "You got a dirty mind, Al."

"Hell, yes," he said. "Who hasn't? O.K. You kids be

good then. No hanky-pank." He waved a finger.

Helen Garden said frostily, "Let's go, Al. If they want a comedian, they can turn on the TV."

He sniffed and winked at me. Helen told me it had been a pleasure making my acquaintance and hoped she would have the pleasure again and they left.

Rita said, "Tell me about Pete."

I told her what had happened and added, "There's a possibility that Pete's death is connected with his cousin's. It might even be that Pete knew who killed Johnny."

Her eyes were thoughtful. "Yeah. That could be." She nodded.

I waited for a clarification, but none came. I asked. "Did he mention something like that to you?"

She paused and then said quietly, "He said the law wasn't seeing what was right in front of their noses. He said he was almost sure he knew who killed Johnny."

"Who?"

She shrugged.

"He told you that much and you weren't interested enough to ask more?"

"I asked. He said it wasn't my business." She gulped. "I had a feeling . . . you know, that Pete was going to take care of it his own way. He . . . was wild at times."

"How long were you with him last night?"

She stared at me suspiciously. "What difference does it make? He was alive when I left him. Drunk, but *alive.*"

"If the police know when you left him, it might help to establish the time of death," I explained.

"Police?" She stiffened, glaring. "Like hell! I thought you were a *private* eye."

"The police are looking for you," I said, "and I have to work with them. We'd better go down to the station now, Rita."

She shook her head stubbornly, backing doubtfully away from me.

"I'll go with you," I said calmly, "and see that you get a square deal. You have to go down, Rita. They asked me to bring you in."

She was breathing heavily again and her voice was labored. "How do I know you're not lying to me? How do I know I'll ever see the station if I go with you?"

"Phone the Police Department," I said. "Ask them if I'm to bring you in. I'll wait outside, if you want me to."

She glanced at the phone and back at me. "Who told you my name?"

"A person who will also tell the police," I lied; "a person who wants to stay out of it."

"Mary Chavez?" she guessed.

"No. Rita, I'm not trying to pressure you and I'll try to prevent the police from pressuring you."

"What does that mean?"

"Oh, they might threaten you with a morals charge if they think you're not being co-operative. They can be rough."

"Morals charge? Who you trying to kid? Pete wasn't married and I'm not. We got a right to date."

"All right," I said wearily. "I'm not here to argue with you. I'll tell the police who and where you are and let them take over. May I use your phone?"

There was a silence of seconds. Then, "How can I tell who's side you're on? You weren't no buddy of Pete's."

"I'm working for a friend of his—for Skip Lund. You can check that, too, if you want to. Phone the station."

Another doubtful silence of about ten seconds. Then she said dully, "Wait here. I'll get a coat."

When she came back to the living room, she was wearing

a beige car coat and I noticed that she kept one hand inside the coat, out of sight.

It wasn't until we were in the car and moving that I learned why that hand had been hidden.

As we passed under a street light the hand came out, and it was holding a long, narrow, sharp and shining bread knife, which glistened malevolently in the reflected light.

"Right for the station," she said hoarsely. "One wrong move out of you and you get it."

I drove carefully and silently, making no wrong moves.

Vogel wasn't there, but Captain Dahl was still in the chief's office. He looked from me to Rita and asked, "Is this the girl?"

I nodded.

"Quick work," he commented. "Will you go out and tell the man at the desk to send in Lynch for dictation? You can wait out there."

"She'd like me to stay with her," I said.

He shook his head. "If she wants a lawyer, she can call one. What's she got to hide?"

"Nothing," Rita said. "What kind of crack was that?"

Dahl looked at her without interest and said to me, "Have Lynch sent in and stay out there." He looked back at Rita. "None of your Constitutional rights are going to be violated here, Miss. You don't need Mr. Callahan present."

Rita Wollard looked between us doubtfully and then said, "O.K., Callahan, I'll talk to him alone. You stay within shouting distance, though."

"I certainly will," I promised. "And if you feel you need a lawyer, you don't have to tell the captain anything until your lawyer gets here."

"I don't want a lawyer," she said. "They're as bad as cops."

"Worse," I said and obediently went out to send in Lynch.

There wasn't any reason why I couldn't have stayed in the room while Dahl took Rita's statement. There wasn't any reason but Dahl's ego. They couldn't find Skip Lund and I had brought him in. And now Rita. His arrogance, like mine, was based on his lacks.

It didn't soften my resentment. I sat on a bench in the hall and watched the man called Lynch go in with his notebook. After about five minutes, I grew bored with sitting on the bench.

I went out to the front room, where the man who had let me see Skip last night was once more in charge of the desk.

He smiled genially. "You mustn't mind the captain's bias. His first wife used a private man to get grounds for a divorce."

"I don't handle divorce work," I said, "and I'm sure he knows it. Has Sergeant Vogel come back from wherever he was?"

He shook his head. "Not yet." He looked around and lowered his voice. "He went over to see Montegro. He's on vacation, but Vogel wonders why he didn't start on his trip. Would you know?"

"I might. Maybe Officer Montegro will be disciplined?"

The man shook his head again. "Montegro is an old and respected name in this town. I'm sure Juan can take care of himself in all ways."

"I'm glad," I said. "He struck me as a very conscientious man and a capable officer."

"Oh, yes." The man sighed. "And we sure as hell could use a few more like him around here."

A traffic officer came in then and I went back to the bench in the hall. The death of Pete Chavez had made the trail to the killer no clearer. So far. To me. I had no way of knowing if it was making the trail clearer to Dahl and

Lynch, in there with Rita. I wondered if they were learning any more from her than I had.

At ten o'clock she came out, her eyes blazing. "Cops!" she said. "The snotty bastards!"

"It's all over," I soothed her. "It's behind you now."

"Let's get out of here," she said. "I hate the smell of the place."

From the open doorway behind her, Dahl said, "Will you come in here a moment, Mr. Callahan?"

I nodded and said to Rita, "Wait in the car if you want the air. I'll be right out."

She went down the hallway as I went back into the chief's office.

Dahl was smiling slightly, a welcome change. He said, "We got off to a bad start, didn't we?"

"Yes."

His voice was humorously dry. "You managed to come up with Lund and now this girl despite that, didn't you?"

I nodded.

"Maybe we need you more than we realize," he said.

I would have felt smug except that this Dahl was too cute. I looked for the angle and said nothing.

"We'll work together from now on," he said. "You keep us informed and our files will be open to you."

"Thank you, Captain," I said humbly, and went out wondering why the wind had shifted.

Perhaps Vogel had reported back and I hadn't seen him. Perhaps he had reported back by phone after talking with Juan Montegro.

In the car Rita Wollard was still miffed. "Cops!" she grumbled.

"Aw, they're not so bad," I said. "There are times when they can be real sweet."

"Phooey!" she said. "Let's get out of here."

We made the trip in silence. I could have asked her what she had told them, but I didn't need to. Their files were open to me, Captain Dahl had said.

In front of her place, as I stopped, she sighed. "Sunday nights. They're the worst, huh? I suppose you have to keep working."

"Unfortunately I do," I double-lied. "Damn it!"

"O.K., O.K.," she said. "I get the message." She opened the door and stepped from the car.

"Wait," I said, and opened the glove compartment.

She turned. Hopefully? She turned, anyway.

I took out the long, narrow, sharp, and glittering bread knife and handed it to her. "You forgot your protection," I said. "Sleep tight."

SIXTEEN

IN MY RENTED room, futility gnawed at me. I was doing as well as or better than the San Valdesto Police Department, but it didn't diminish my sense of insufficiency. I was on a cold trail.

Was there an alternate trail?

Pablo Chun had said, "Johnny was always in hot water. . . . If it wasn't money, it was women."

Love and money, lust and greed. . . .

I undressed slowly and climbed into bed, shivering for no reason at all except the general state of the world. Love or money. . . .

It had been love for June and money had almost destroyed it. It had been money with Glenys and love came late and fraudulently. With Jan the money didn't stop the love but the lack of it prevented the marriage. That dopey Jan. . . .

In the warm bed I stayed cold, tossing, fretful, as tag ends of dialogue came to me, remembrances of attitudes and slights, of humiliations and small successes.

Damn it, I was too dumb for this business! Big enough, but too dumb. I dozed and saw Mary Chavez looking up at me, Bud Lund looking up at me, and the horizontal Glenys looking up at me. To hell with all of them. Except Bud.

I dozed and began to perspire, still chilled. I fell asleep.

I wakened suddenly. I was still perspiring, still chilled, but now I was also frightened. From the black-top parking area behind my room came the sound of a stealthy footstep. I tensed, listening for another.

I heard a voice mumbling incoherently and then the scrape of another footstep. Some drunk coming home?

My peasant's prescience assured me that it was not that innocent.

I slipped quickly and quietly out of bed and over to my valise holding the .38. I took it with me as I padded in my bare feet to the door and pressed one ear against it.

I could hear hoarse breathing now and then the scratch of a match and a whispered, "Ah!"

There was a muffled knock.

"Who's there?" I asked softly.

"Open up, you bastard!" the voice said—the voice of Lars Hovde.

I opened the door. He had a jacket over his sport shirt; otherwise, his uniform was the same. Something glistened in his right hand and I brought the gun up quickly.

It was a bottle. I lowered the gun.

"What's wrong, Red?" I asked quietly.

"You're wrong," he said. "You stay away from that Juanita, you understand?"

"Come in," I said, "and keep your voice down. People are trying to sleep."

He studied me warily and came in. I closed the door behind him and tried not to inhale the odor of wine that had come in with him.

I asked quietly, "Who gave you my address?"

He grinned slyly. "I'll ask the questions, peeper. Why

you bothering Juanita? You leave her alone, see?"

I lifted the gun and he must have seen it for the first time. His face grew even uglier and he stared at me without any visible fear. "What the hell's that for? Put it away, gutless."

I shook my head. "Who sent you here, Red? Not Juanita."

"Never mind who sent me. Put that goddamned gun away!" He raised the bottle in his hand, an empty wine bottle, a quart.

He was too drunk to be scared. I kept the gun on him. I said quietly, "I think the edge is mine. I've used this gun. I don't like to, but I have. You're trespassing, Red, and I'll use it if I have to. Once more now—who sent you here?"

He pointed at his belly with a thumb. "*I* sent me here. And that gun don't scare me. I'm warning you, Irish—"

I lifted the gun higher and extended my arm. The business end of the barrel was now about a foot from his nose. I said, "Shut up!"

It was probably not fear that came to his glazed eyes—only the beginning of caution. He was momentarily silent.

"Who sent you?" I asked again. "This wasn't your idea, coming here, and it wasn't Juanita's. She and I are working together."

"Huh!" he said. "You don't fool me."

"Nobody does," I said patiently, "but you're mistaken if you think I won't shoot you. I want some answers, Red."

He dropped the empty bottle on the carpeted floor and it came rolling and bouncing my way.

I said, "Don't move. I'm calling the police." I kept the gun on him and took half a step toward the phone.

"Huh!" he said once more, and turned his back to me, heading for the rear door.

"Stay where you are," I said, but he kept moving.

He opened the door and turned. "You don't fool me," he said once more. "You ain't got the guts to pull the trigger."

He went out and slammed the door behind him.

I stood there for a few seconds, shaking and wet. Then I went to the door and opened it. I could see him in the overhead light, walking toward the darkness of the highway.

Then a pair of headlights went on down there and Red disappeared into the shadows. I heard the slam of a car door and saw the headlights begin to move, but it was too dark for me to identify the car.

And then, from the south, another pair of headlights came along and illuminated the car that was leaving. It was an ancient and faded two-door Rambler.

Those lights had gone on before Red had reached the car. So somebody had been waiting for him. It might have been the somebody who knew where I was staying; it could have been the somebody who had prompted Red's irrational visit.

I closed the door again and locked it and put my gun back in my bag. In the bathroom I washed my sticky face.

I considered phoning the police but decided that I could tell them about it tomorrow. I checked the front-door lock and went back to bed.

It must have been one o'clock before I finally fell asleep.

Monday dawned hot and dry, perfect tourist weather. I went to Headquarters from the downtown restaurant where I had eaten breakfast.

Captain Dahl, in a smaller office, was gloomy and pessimistic. He said, "No match for the print and no gun for the slug. Maybe Washington can help us on the print." He took a deep breath.

I said, "A fingerprint will be mighty handy *after* we find a killer. And that .30-.30 slug might be, too. Could I see your file on Johnny Chavez?"

He sighed. "I don't know what you could find there. No lead that I can see. Sergeant Cloda will show it to you."

He looked at me bleakly. "You keep us informed, now, at all times."

"Absolutely," I said, and went to look up Sergeant Cloda.

It was a skimpy file. But it was also more than that. It lacked a story I had heard, a throwaway line. I tried to remember—hadn't Vogel told me about the knifing?

And then I remembered. It had been Deputy Dunphy, up in Solvang.

I asked Sergeant Cloda, "Doesn't your Department co-operate with the Sheriff's Department on exchange of information on local citizens?"

He nodded, frowning. "Why? Something missing from that file?"

"I heard something from Deputy Dunphy that isn't in here."

"If Dunphy had a record of it, we'd have it. Was it a rumor or a *fact?* I mean, of course, an *official* fact."

"Maybe it was a rumor. I don't know. I'll have to check with Dunphy, I guess." I put the file back. "Could I use your phone to call Solvang?"

I could and I did, but Dunphy was not in his office. I went back in to see Dahl.

I told him, "Wasn't Johnny Chavez knifed once, or threatened with a knife? Dunphy, up at Solvang, told me something like that."

Dahl rubbed the back of his neck and put down the papers he'd been studying. "If it's not in his file, we have no record of it. Do you think it could be important?"

"Maybe not. Lacking anything solid, I'm looking for straws." I paused. "You know, the way Vogel came charging into what should have been a county case, there's a possibility that we're lacking important information."

"Easy, now," he said. "I know you don't like Vogel much, but let's not use him as a whipping boy."

I hesitated and then said, "I'll tell you somebody else who doesn't like Vogel—Deputy Gerald Dunphy."

The bright-blue eyes began to frost. "Any police officer worth his salt works with any other police officer whether he likes him or not. Both Dunphy and Vogel are first-class officers."

"But also human beings," I said. "Dunphy has a right to resent the way Vogel took over." I paused. "Because of his pal Ritter."

Silence. Captain Dahl was angry, I could tell. But I had a hunch he was also thinking hard, digesting what I'd said.

I added quietly, "I'm not being arrogant or malicious. I'm simply trying to explain why there might be a gap in our knowledge on Johnny Chavez."

After about ten seconds of silence, he said, "It's Monday. Dunphy could be at the courthouse. He often is, on Mondays. Why don't you run over there?"

It was only a block away; I walked over. Dunphy was in town as Dahl had guessed, but he was in court and not available until noon.

I went back and reported that to the captain. He said, "Maybe you and Vogel could meet him for lunch and see if there are any gaps." He smiled.

"Wouldn't that be cozy?" I commented. "Why don't I meet Dunphy without the help of Vogel? It would probably make all three of us happier."

"A good suggestion," he said. "I'm glad to see you're finally working with the Department. Carry on, Callahan."

He was a cutie, that Dahl. He was undoubtedly the Department comedian, in his dry way. But how was his loyalty? I had helped him. When the time came, would he remember that?

And would the time come that I might need him? What was I working on? A hunch, an instinct, a nothing. Routine and detail—that was the municipal route. It was the most efficient way to function. It took men and equipment and leg work—and *all* the details.

Because of Vogel's desire to move into this case involving his buddy's married loved one, one of the details could have been lost in transference. There was no reason to think it was an important detail.

I sat in the courthouse park, watching the pudgy tourists photograph this prime example of Spanish architecture, waiting for noon and lunch with Dunphy. I had left a message for him to meet me at a nearby restaurant.

Because of Dahl, I was finally feeling like a citizen. Because of Montegro, I had gained the forced acceptance of Dahl. But they were still cops—and I wasn't. I hadn't forgotten that.

Finding the killer of Johnny Chavez wouldn't get Skip off the hook they hoped to keep him on. But it would force them to make a new decision—a new charge on which to hold Skip. And then I would need a reasonable enemy if I couldn't find a friend in the Department.

Dahl might never be a friend, but he was beginning to shape up as a reasonable enemy.

Deputy Gerald Dunphy was waiting in the bar for me when I got to the restaurant. He smiled and said, "I was surprised to learn you were still in town. Get a new client, did you?"

"The man I was looking for decided to hire me. I'm working for Lund and *with* the San Valdesto Police Department, finally."

"Oh? And the great Vogel has decided he needs county help?"

"No. This was my idea. Let's go in and get a table."

When we were seated in the restaurant, Dunphy said, "I don't know how I can be of any help. The Department here has everything we have on Johnny Chavez. We don't have anything on his cousin."

"It was a remark you made," I said, "in your office. You mentioned someone who had attacked Johnny Chavez with a knife."

He frowned and I thought his face looked guarded.

I tried to recall his words in that hot office. "Let's see . . . you said something about bar fights and then—oh, I remember. A woman whose husband had a knife."

"So?" Dunphy said.

"So there's no record of a knifing of Johnny Chavez at San Valdesto Headquarters and I wondered about it."

Dunphy said quietly, "We haven't any record of it either." He seemed embarrassed. "That was some time ago. I . . . happened to be around, though not on duty, that Sunday when this husband tried to knife Chavez. I didn't think it should go on the kid's record; he already had enough strikes against him."

"Logical enough," I agreed. "But what was the man's name?"

Dunphy stared at the table and then up at me. "So help me, I've forgotten it."

I sighed.

"It was a nothing," he insisted, "a two-minute incident. You're not thinking it has any connection with his murder, are you?"

"There's not much reason to think so." I paused. "Except that the police down here have kept an eye on Johnny for a long time. And with all that background they've come up with absolutely no lead. So we're looking for leads they didn't have. This was one of those."

The waitress came and we ordered. Dunphy was lost in thought.

I said, "All I have now is an accumulation of remarks from people that were dropped during my questioning and that didn't seem related to the trail we were on. That one about the husband and the knife was one."

"And what happened last night—does that fit in?"

"Pete," I said, "was probably looking for Johnny's killer. He made a remark to a girl friend that the law wasn't seeing what was right under their noses. Well, the law doesn't overlook the obvious. So it occurred to me that what Pete thought the law knew had never been recorded."

Dunphy said, "I'm almost sure I can find out the man's name for you. I remember some other people who were there now and they'll know his name. I think it was Jose. I'll check those people. Where can I phone you?"

"I don't know. Couldn't I phone you?"

He would be in court until two-thirty and he would need an hour after that, he estimated. He gave me a phone number where he could be reached at four o'clock.

That was three hours from now, and I decided to look up Lars Hovde while I waited.

At Headquarters they had Red's home address and the name of the place where he was employed. It was the lumberyard near the home of Mary Chavez.

The manager there told me that Lars had phoned this morning and reported himself too sick to work. "He quite often does," the manager added, "on Mondays. I only put up with the slob because he's such a demon worker when he's sober."

At the rooming house where Lars lived his landlady told me, "He was in bed until one o'clock. Then he said he had to go out and get some medicine."

Medicine, eighty-six proof, blended. . . . I asked, "Does he drive a Rambler?"

"He don't drive nothing," she said scornfully. "The law took away his driver's license and the finance company took away his car six months ago. He don't drive nothing and he ain't got nothing."

I thanked her and left.

There was no other place to go. I wouldn't have any new hope until four o'clock, and that could prove to be nothing. I headed the flivver toward Montevista.

Pete, I kept reminding myself, had known Johnny longer than Skip had. Pete had been familiar with Johnny's old loves and new. And his steady love?

Under the overhanging trees in peaceful Montevista the flivver chugged along. She seemed to turn almost automatically between the stucco pillars.

There were three landscape men working in the front yard and an improvement was already visible. On the front porch June Christopher Lund was sitting with a cup of coffee, overseeing the work. She smiled as I came along the walk from the parking area.

"You're the foreman," I guessed.

"Right. I want it nice for Skip when he comes home. And he's coming home, isn't he?"

"We live in hope."

She smiled confidently. She turned to call through the open window behind her. "Glenys, your boy friend is here." She turned back to grin maliciously. "You caught her with her hair down and no Einlicher in the refrigerator."

"You shouldn't tease her," I said. "She's a real citizen."

"I've always teased her. You can go right in."

In the living room Glenys was going through a stack of phonograph records, arranging them in two piles. She was wearing blue jeans and a T shirt and there was a long streak of dust on her forearm.

"Coon-Saunders," she said, "and their Kansas City Night-hawks. Have you ever heard of them?"

"I remember Joe Saunders," I said, "but the original band was before my time." I nodded toward the front yard. "Your idea?"

"June's. She no longer needs an Aunt Glenys—not with Uncle Brock around. Do you like warm Einlicher?"

"At this price I can drink it warm."

She went out and came back with two bottles, one for her and one for me. She sat down near me and said acidly, "I see another of Skip's dear friends was killed last night. Well, at least the hot-rodder can't be blamed for that murder."

"Easy, now, Aunt Glenys. Skip's in enough trouble without having family enemies."

"He'll be clear now, won't he?"

"I don't know. He's in trouble. I have one small, last hope of finding the murderer, but he'll still be in trouble. If I find the murderer, I'll have to stop investigating and turn into a politician. I'm not very good at that."

Her eyes narrowed. "Politician? Does that mean . . . a . . . a *deal?*"

"In a way. It's too complicated to explain and I would have to betray a trust to make it clear. Let's talk about something else."

Her chin lifted. "What shall we talk about?" A pause. "Jan?"

I flushed. She did, too.

She sipped her beer. "Damn you! I'll get a man even bigger than you. And one with some class—a *halfback!*"

I grinned at her. "I know one like that, and he's rich and single, too. His name is Scooter Calvin. I'll bring him around some night when you're back in civilization. He's lighter than I am, but better looking and taller."

"Oh, shut up!" she said, but there was no venom in her voice.

We talked about other things then. When Bud came home from school and learned that his Aunt Glenys had planned to throw away all his Coon-Saunders records, we had a temporary domestic crisis.

And then it was time to call Dunphy.

≋≋≋≋≋ *SEVENTEEN* ≋≋≋≋≋

THE HUB AND nub of it had been here all the time. At Chickie's, where the queen reigned. I stood in the hot, late-afternoon sun in front of her place and saw the faded, ancient Rambler parked about half a block up the street, under the shade of a eucalyptus.

I went up the steps slowly and into the dim coolness. The blind on the largest window had been lowered and it was dark in the bar. The guitar player and one of his buddies were playing gin rummy at a table near the kitchen door. There were no customers.

"Mrs. Rico here?" I asked.

The guitar player nodded and inclined his head toward the kitchen door. "She's busy now."

"Who's out there?" Juanita called. "Is that Pancho Callahan?"

"Right."

"Come back," she called. "I can't come out; my hands are full of flour."

The boys at the table said something in Spanish as I pushed through the swinging door. I came into a small, cluttered, dark, but well-scrubbed kitchen. There was a light directly over Juanita's head and her lustrous hair glinted. She was kneading dough.

Her smile was innocent and cordial. "What's new?"

"Most of it's old," I said. "As old as time. You never told me you and Johnny Chavez were lovers, Juanita."

She stopped working. Her brown eyes went toward the swinging door and then came back to rest sadly on me. "Not so loud. Who told you that?"

"You didn't; that's what is important. Your husband tried to knife Johnny once, didn't he? So your husband must have known what was going on."

She shook her head. "Jose was drunk that day. Since that day he has never again mentioned the name of Johnny Chavez."

"But he knew about it. Last night he brought Red Hovde over to my motel room. That's Jose's Rambler up the street, isn't it?"

She nodded. "Why would he bring Red over?"

"Maybe he thought Red was big enough and drunk enough to scare me off. He knew about you and Johnny, Juanita. And he killed him. Does he still have the rifle?"

"Damn you," she whispered, "not so loud. I have the guns. Jose has no guns."

"A knife, though? He used it on Pete because Pete knew what was going on. But out in the open country it's not easy to creep up on a man with a knife. So he used one of your rifles. There's a slug down at Headquarters waiting to be matched to your rifle, Juanita."

"No," she whispered, but there was doubt on her face. "Never!"

"They jumped Red, too—Jose and his friends—didn't they?"

The doubt grew in her face and she looked at me fearfully.

I asked. "Do you live in this building?"

She nodded.

"Get me the .30-.30 then. I'll take it down to Headquarters and we can check it out."

"Jose," she said softly, "has not fired a gun since he was a boy. He wouldn't . . . he couldn't . . . he plays cards, he plays the guitar, he is happy. No!"

"Get the gun," I said. "And I'll take Jose down to Head-quarters. There's a fingerprint that needs matching, too—a fingerprint in blood from the doorknob of Skip Lund's apart-ment. The blood is the blood of Pete Chavez. And the fingerprint could be Jose's."

"No," she said. "We can't have the police in my business. If Jose is guilty—"

"The police must know," I finished for her. "You're not an executioner, Juanita. There is no other way."

From the barroom I heard a door close. The front door. And then there was a shade being pulled. Juanita looked doubtfully at me. The big shade had been down; what shade was being pulled now?

She stared at the swinging door.

"The shade on the door?" I asked quietly. "The shade that says 'Closed' on it when it's down?"

She was breathing heavily, staring at the motionless swinging door.

I said, "He was playing cards when I came in. I think he has now sent his friend home and locked the front door. I guess he overheard us, Juanita."

"Wait," she said hoarsely. She wiped her hands on her apron. "You wait here."

I thought she was going into the bar, but she headed for another door, a door that probably led to their living quarters.

I stood near the big triple sink, cursing my inadequacy. I had come here directly from Montevista, not going back to the motel for my .38.

When I had left the motel this morning, there hadn't seemed to be any need for a gun; it was now safely locked in my valise.

Quietly I moved over toward the doorway through which Juanita had disappeared.

And then, from the other room, I heard the ring of the phone and I waited. I heard his voice, the quiet voice of the matriarch's husband, the dominated man named Jose Rico. The guitar man.

He spoke too low for me to hear, but then he called, "Mr. Callahan, it's for you. It's Sergeant Vogel."

Vogel? How would he know I was here? Well, maybe. . . . I said, "I'll be there in a second." But I stood where I was.

In a few seconds he swung the door open and stood half in the kitchen, half out, holding the door open with his back. There was nothing in either of his hands, and no noticeable bulge was in his pockets.

He said quietly, "Sergeant Vogel says it's important."

"Thank you."

I went past him warily, wondering about Juanita, keeping Jose in sight peripherally as I walked to the phone behind the bar.

I still had Jose in sight as I picked up the phone. It was a dead line.

I said, "Now your friend is involved, too. You had him phone, didn't you? That makes him an accomplice."

He shrugged and smiled. He walked to the other end of the bar and reached a hand underneath it. When the hand came out, there was a gun in it, a big service automatic, a .45.

His voice was soft and musical. "Pete is dead. Johnny is dead. Adulterers, both. Home wreckers, men of violence and no substance. They are better off dead."

"It was murder," I said. "You can't change that."

"Nor bring them back to life. How much money do you want?"

I stalled, hoping for time, hoping for the return of Juanita. I stalled and pretended to be considering his question.

"How much?" he asked again.

I said doubtfully, "Juanita wouldn't stand still for murder. She wouldn't let you buy me off."

"Juanita," he said quietly, "will not spoil her charity work with police. Juanita needs me and I her and we are wasting time."

"Let's wait until she gets here," I said. "We'll talk it over, the three of us."

His eyes smoldered in suspicion and he said, "Come out from behind the bar; come out in the open where I can see you have no gun."

Out in the open, where he could get a shot at me. Out in the open, where I couldn't dive for cover if he missed the first shot.

I stayed where I was.

"Move!" he said softly. "Move now!"

Slowly I moved around the end of the bar, keeping an eye on the tables, looking for one with a chair missing, a table I could get under in one dive if I saw his trigger finger tightening.

He came around from his end of the bar, the big blue-black gun steady in his bony hand, his soft eyes appraising me carefully, his long face showing no emotion but his wariness.

And then, in that lost second, the swinging door from the kitchen swung in violently our way and Juanita came through it like the hero in a Western movie.

There was no puny automatic in her capable hands. It took both her hands to carry the double-barreled twelve-gauge shotgun that was now pointed at the belly of her soft-voiced, guitar-playing husband.

"Put it away, Jose," she said steadily. "Drop your little pistol on the floor."

He smiled and shook his head. "You would not shoot me. And if I get rid of him, you will not tell the police. Our friends would suffer if you turned me over to the police."

"Drop it, Jose," she repeated sharply. "I will shoot. You killed Johnny and I will shoot if you don't drop that gun."

He turned to stare at her, surprise on his face. She shouldn't have mentioned Johnny. Adultery he could understand, but not her preferring Johnny.

I picked a table I thought I could make. He turned from her to me again, just as I was ready to dive, and his face was harder now and there was hate in his dreamy eyes.

"Drop it, damn you!" she said.

This time the shake of his head was final and my eyes dropped to his hand. The trigger finger was starting to tighten.

I dived.

I heard the whine of the slug past my ear and then the smashing blast of that .45 was engulfed in a tidal wave of sound, the near-atomic boom of *both* twelve-gauge barrels going off at the same time in a closed room.

My ears would ring every time I thought of that afternoon.

"Sweep him up?" the officer said to Dahl. "We had to *mop* him up, Captain. He caught both barrels in the belly, full choke. Even the intern got sick."

We were in Dahl's small office. A uniformed man came in and said, "That .30-.30 checks out. Her gun, but she swears she hasn't used it in a year."

I looked at Vogel. Vogel looked out the window. Dahl looked at the uniformed man and said, "Jose probably used it. How about that fingerprint?"

"Terris is checking it. He should know by now."

The man named Terris came in before the sentence was completed. He said, "Thumbprint checks out. Thank God he had a thumb left. And he handled that .30-.30, too. At least he cleaned it. His prints are on it in oil."

Terris went out and the uniformed man went out.

Vogel and Dahl and I were now alone. I asked innocently, "Where's Chief Harris? Shouldn't he be here?"

Vogel muttered something. Dahl's smile was cynical. "Don't get cute, Callahan; you're not holding that good a hand."

"I haven't made any bets," I said. "What happens now?"

"What do you want to happen?" he asked me frankly. "If I cover for Lund, I have to cover for Mrs. Rico, too. She killed a man, Callahan."

"Saving my life," I said. "He shot first."

Sergeant Bernard Vogel said unctuously, "Is it Department policy, Captain, to make deals with private investigators?"

Dahl looked at the sergeant bleakly and ominously. "You favor holding Lund on some other charge, is that it, Sergeant? You're willing to ride that out?"

Vogel hesitated. He had a deuce in the hole and I didn't blame him.

Dahl looked at me. "You going to bat for your girl friend, too—is that it?"

"My girl friend?"

"You know who I mean. Juanita Rico."

"She's not my girl friend, Captain, and I think she's perfectly capable of taking care of herself. I just want to take Skip Lund home to his family. I will then get the hell out of your rough town."

I thought there was relief in Dahl's sigh. He looked at

Vogel. Vogel shrugged, carefully not looking at me.

Dahl said, "You brought us in a killer. I guess we owe you something for that. We might *never* have found him."

Vogel went over to look out the window.

I said, "I was paid to bring in a killer by my client. He's a different man now. He'll undoubtedly sell that boat and get back into the filling-station business. He'll go back to his wife, I know. That won't make your ex-mayor happy, but we can't have everything, can we?"

Vogel turned from the window to stare at me. I glanced at him and said to Dahl, "All I want to do is get out of here. This is the first Department in a long time where I was treated as a criminal. The taste of it is still in my mouth."

Dahl smiled. "I love it when you sulk. How often do we see a two-hundred-and-fifty-pound tiger sulking?"

I stood up. "Take a good look; you'll never see me again. Well . . . ?"

Dahl said to Vogel, "Go tell them to release Lund and bring him here."

Vogel went out. Dahl said, "So we didn't trust you. Any time you want a recommendation from this Department, have the inquiry addressed to me." He held out a hand.

I shook it. I said, "We're friends only because I had an ace in the hole, aren't we?"

"Maybe," he admitted. "That's the best kind, isn't it?" He turned serious. "And keep your lip off Vogel on the way out. He's still one hell of a fine officer."

"Of course, Captain," I said humbly. "Of course."

The sun was slanting through the eucalypti. In my flivver, Skip Lund opened the window on his side and took a deep breath of the hot, dry air.

"God, that smells good," he said. He lighted a cigarette. "Man, the clink is not for me."

"Remember it. And watch your temper. Maybe grow up a little, huh?"

"Yes, Uncle Brock," he said. "What's this I hear about you and Glenys?"

"We're old friends. Anything else you heard is nonsense." I turned in between the stucco pillars.

"Look at that yard!" he said. "When did they start working on that?"

"Today," I said.

And then, from the garage, I saw my former client on his bike and he saw us, and he dropped the bike and started to streak across the lawn.

"Stop," Skip said, and I slowed to stop, but he had the door open before we were motionless and he was running across to pick up his kid.

I left the car there, and stood for a second, but neither of them was thinking of me. I walked up toward the house, resentful and jealous.

Then Glenys came out onto the porch and she, too, stood for a moment, watching the damp reunion.

"Hello," I said.

She came down to where I stood. "Won't you stay for dinner? Bud will want you to, I'm sure, as soon as he comes to his senses."

June came down from the porch and ran past us, toward her family.

Glenys put a hand on my arm. And I thought, *Right now, she's as lonely as I am.*

"You will stay, won't you?" she asked softly.

The hand on my arm tightened.

I said carefully, "Thank you, but I have to get back to town. I've already picked up my clothes and checked out of the motel."

Her grip loosened slightly.

"But," I added, "I'd appreciate it if you'd phone Jan and tell her I'm on the way home. Tell her to wait and we'll have a late dinner at Cini's."

Her hand went away. She nodded agreement.

I climbed into the flivver and started the engine. The trio on the lawn were all looking my way now, and Skip called something, but I didn't stop.

I waved my goodbye and went out the driveway to the road. The flivver seemed to steer herself, sighing happily, heading for home.